# IN EXCESS OF DARK

### RED LAGOE

SOBELO BOOKS

ISBN (Ebook): 978-1-965389-02-7
ISBN (Paperback): 978-1-965389-03-4

# PRAISE FOR IN EXCESS OF DARK

"A somber and deeply upsetting escalation of weirdness, Red Lagoe's *In Excess of Dark* is a serrated examination of love, loss, and death. These elements intertwine flawlessly in a disturbing vision of grief from a fresh and audacious voice in horror fiction."
- **Eric LaRocca, author of *Things Have Gotten Worse Since We Last Spoke***

"Like Pet Sematary before it, *In Excess of Dark* is a sad and often shocking meditation on the devastating impact of grief. It's also Red Lagoe's finest book to date--a terrifying tale of loss and hereditary darkness that will keep you enthralled right up to the shocking, skin-crawling conclusion."
- **Kealan Patrick Burke, Bram Stoker Award®-winning author of *Kin* and *Sour Candy***

"*In Excess of Dark* is an intense examination of grief and regret that tiptoes along the borderland of creativity and madness. Lagoe pulls no punches here. The ending will knock the wind out of you."
– **Todd Keisling, Bram Stoker Award®-nominated author of *Devil's Creek* and *Scanlines***

"*In Excess of Dark* is a dark, tightly written journey through the nightmare of an all-too relatable mind. Red Lagoe has crafted a fast-paced tale of inner darkness, casting a light on the shadows we all carry. Karina's slid into guilt and despair is woven with brutal and increasing terror, written with Lagoe's deft touch for scene, atmosphere and emotion. A fantastic novella."
– **Laurel Hightower, author of *Silent Key, Crossroads,* and *Below***

# ALSO BY RED LAGOE

*Impulses of a Necrotic Heart*
*Lucid Screams*
*Dismal Dreams*

# Content Warning

The story that follows explores, in excess, themes of loss, grief and suicidal ideations.
Several scenes also depict graphic violence and gore.
Reader discretion is advised.

# Contents

# DEDICATION

*To Jason, Niam, and Jack:*
*Without you, I'd be lost forever to the darkness.*

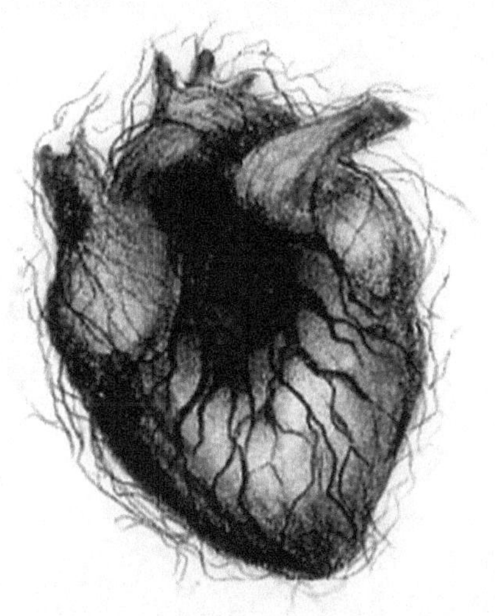

# Chapter 1

Some people feel a void when someone they love is gone, but for Karina, she felt her father's presence. Not in a ghostly, ethereal kind of way. Instead, all the good memories, all the fun, the lessons, the late-night pizza parties, the heart-to-heart talks...all the *love*...it didn't stay inside her as a light in the darkness. It withered. It rotted. Much like their relationship had over the years. And now all the stink and decay of his old existence was locked inside her, fumes accumulating. Seams of her flesh bulging from the buildup within. However, if she could've drilled holes in her body to relieve the pressure, she wasn't sure she would. Because then he'd be gone completely, released as nothing more than a gaseous hiss to the night.

A bone-deep ache thrummed in her body at the thought. A year since his passing, and there wasn't a day she didn't miss him. A cliché phrase spewed by millions of grieving people. *There wasn't a day I didn't miss him.*

Really? Not even a day? Every day of every year, you thought about that loved one? Karina didn't believe it until it had happened to her. Until fate in the shape of a heart attack claimed a healthy man in his fifties. Next, the first stroke struck him down, and his health spiraled into oblivion.

The universe is a harsh motherfucker, an expanse of nothingness devouring light, but her dad had taught her to seek those pinpoints of light, to reach for them and hold on for dear life.

He taught her that sometimes it's so dark and cold, nothing else matters. Family become rogue planets drifting lightyears away, and it feels like there's no way back to them. So why even try? And sometimes, you open your eyes, and your people are right next to you. A source of life, and you're safe within their gravity.

Sunlight shone through the car window, and she pulled her passenger-side visor down to protect her eyes from the painful glare. Her husband, Gavin, was at the wheel, approaching the mountainside's sharp switchbacks at speeds she thought were a little too fast, even for an uphill climb. Breaks squealed each time they neared a corner.

"Can you slow down?" She seized the grab handle.

"We're fine." Gavin pressed the accelerator and the old Accord lurched to a higher RPM. A pickup truck roared toward them in the opposite lane; its wind current shook their small car as it whipped by. Behind, the pickup's brake lights glowed hot red as it flew toward the sharp corner they'd just navigated. She pictured it flying off the edge of the mountain and tumbling down.

Her son, Xander, sat in the backseat. Unfazed by the passing vehicle, his lifeless eyes crawled across his open sketchbook. Thick pencil sketches of monsters adorned the pages. Insect-like appendages and gnashing teeth. Saliva. The blood was drawn in red ink, the only color splashing the page. Xander was an artist, much like his grandfather. If only they'd had more time together.

Behind them, down the mountain, the speeding truck made the turn at the switchback without issue. The return drive would be Hell. They'd have to take this winding road down the mountainside to get back to I-81. Gavin's car was twelve years old and overdue for a new set of brake pads. It should have been handled before they left for their weekend away, but he never got around to it.

The brakes screeched again as they approached another turn. How far down the mountainside did the squealing sound carry? Could the people in the tiny, speck-sized houses hear it? Did it carry through the trees? Or did the budding spring branches absorb it like a sponge soaking up a spill? Would those branches catch their car as it flew off the side of the mountain when their brakes inevitably give out on the downhill trip? The Honda, brake pads smoking, would launch like a daredevil driver over the edge of a sharp corner. The trees were sparse enough that she was certain the car would soar for a while before taking a nosedive toward the ground. Momentum would work against Gavin's attempt to stop, pulling their car violently down the rocky slope. Maybe then Xander would finally look up from his sketchbook and notice the world around him. Maybe his eyes would show something other than apathy—even if it was fear of dying. Her husband wouldn't look her in the face as the forest of underbrush and thorns and moss-ridden logs mangled the tin can car. He'd clench white-knuckled fists on the wheel, right foot smashed into the brake pedal as if he was strong enough to defy gravity. Her purse would spill its contents. Cold coffees would tip. A sketchbook of demons and monsters and blood would hit the ceiling of the car. And they would crash into a massive pine, older and fatter than any in the entire span of the Appalachians. But it wouldn't hit head-on. They'd flip mid-air after bouncing off a rocky outcrop, and the roof of the car would smash parallel with the unforgiving tree. The driver side would take the most damage. Karina would open her eyes and find her husband's skull crushed by the impact. Bits of brain and flesh clinging to the fabric on the car ceiling. In the backseat, Xander's face would be frosted in crimson. Eyes no longer bulging with fear. They'd bulge—nearly out of his head—returning to their expression of apathy, lifeless once again.

The brakes screeched on another switchback and Karina released a held breath, snapping out of the nightmarish daydream. "That noise is so annoying."

"I meant to get it fixed," Gavin said.

"You mean to do a lot of things."

"What's that supposed to mean?" Gavin looked at her.

"Jesus, Gavin. Watch the road." Karina turned away to look out the window.

The image of their dead faces remained, painted in red and fleshy pinks on the canvas of her memory. Something had always been wrong with her mind, the gruesome thoughts it conjured. They were part of her, but whenever she shared her twisted imaginings, it only made people uncomfortable or upset. So, Karina did what she had always done, and she took the blood-smeared painting of her dead family and hung it within her darkest interiors.

Dense trees whizzed by in the foreground, and the steep incline eased to a gradual slope with fewer sharp corners as they neared the top of the mountain range. Deep within the trees, amidst the soft pale green of new spring growth, a black shape caught her eye. It was large and upright, and being in bear country, she was excited to see one in the wild.

But it wasn't a bear. As the foreground blurred by, it was difficult to focus on. It lacked form, yet there was a fluidity to it, or perhaps a nebulosity. She couldn't quite make out its face or which direction it looked, but somehow, she felt like it was aware of her.

# Chapter 2

"Did you see that?" She twisted backward as they rounded a gentle curve, leaving the apparition behind them.

Gavin gave a half-assed glance in the rearview mirror but didn't bother to ask what she'd seen. Xander closed his sketchbook. He crossed his arms. Black leather bracelets with skulls clicked together. His shaggy dark curls, reminiscent of hers, clung to his forehead as he closed his eyes, pretending not to hear. The gap between them grew each day, but this camping trip would save her family. She didn't know in her heart but always imagined Gavin would've been happier with someone else, someone *better*. And she knew Xander was counting the seconds until he could move away from her. This trip was their last chance to come together again as a family. To find each other's light in the darkness.

The campground was primitive. No showers. No electricity. No hookups.

"No signal," Xander said, waggling his phone.

"At least there's a bathroom!" She could still hear her dad's voice in her head, trying to convince Mom they'd be fine for two nights in the woods. They came to this campground every other summer to *rough it* when she was a kid. Karina wanted to return for years, to give Xander a version of her childhood, but he revolted. He wanted nothing to do with the things she enjoyed: camping, quiet, solitude. So when he pushed back, her only defense was to push harder. So much time pushing. Pushing him to do well in school, pushing him to be more outgoing...pushing him to be *more*...all so he'd grow up to be someone who wasn't completely and utterly screwed up.

He grew angrier and distant, and now, going into senior year, it finally dawned on Karina that she should've let him be who he is. She should've been there for him while he figured life out. That's the thing about parenting, by the time you figure out what you've done wrong, it's too late.

Xander and Gavin claimed two camp chairs around a fire pit.

"This is boring," Xander said to the sketchbook in his lap.

"Hey!" Gavin didn't look up from the fire. "Your mom never gets to do what she wants to do, so we can give her one weekend. Last year we went to New York. That was *my* trip. This time, it's your mom's."

"When do I get to pick?"

"When you have a job and pay for it." Gavin chuckled.

"Sooo…" Xander twisted around in his seat and looked toward the paved path by the campsite. Twiggy branches with small green buds lacking foliage offered a clear view down the hillside campground. Only a few other campers were set up on the grounds. "What's there to do other than look at nature?"

Karina tossed some blankets in the tent. "Tomorrow morning, we'll climb Sharp Top Mountain."

Xander raised his eyebrows. "Mountain climbing?"

"It's just a hiking trail up a really big hill, and there's a great view from the top."

"Greeeeat. So, we can look at nature while we walk in nature and when we get to the top, we'll look at more nature?"

Gavin stood up. "And we can piss in nature!" He marched toward the edge of the campsite to relieve himself. "Maybe marking our territory will scare the bears away. Stay away bears!" He shouted into the woods, thrusting his pelvis.

Xander sank like a sagging pillow, embarrassed that someone somewhere in the forest might hear.

Sometimes she forgot why she fell in love with Gavin so many years ago. But moments like this reminded her. They were two silly, young Navy sailors stationed to the same amphib, and they clicked. They made each other happy; he made *her* happy. And *happy* was unfamiliar territory for Karina until adulthood. As a child, as a teenager, she could not see beyond the darkness her mother claimed was inside of her, as it was inside her father.

When Dad passed, the darkness unfurled its many limbs, seizing more and more space within her. Gavin was her rock during the hard times, and she sometimes forgot how much she loved him. Especially when she let the negativity take over. Then the bad thoughts would come. She'd worry about losing them. She'd see impossible scenarios of rogue asteroids, armed robberies, and graphic deadly accidents. Guilt replaced the blood in her heart every time she imagined something terrible happening to her husband, but she didn't have much control over where her mind went.

When Xander fell asleep in his separate tent, they climbed into theirs and zipped it up quietly. The mood wasn't there much lately for Karina, but Gavin had been patient. Occasionally hinting, but never pushing for sex. She knew he wouldn't stray to another woman, but she also knew he wanted to. She'd dreamed of doing it herself. But that evening, her thoughts were only on repairing their relationship.

Scant light entered through an unzipped window screen. A starless sky, snaking black branches silhouetted against it. It was so dark she couldn't even see Gavin's face as he closed in to kiss her. His body was a silhouette as his hands explored the familiar terrain of her body.

She missed the feeling, the warmth, the intensity, but with Xander sleeping less than ten feet away, she held her breath and bottled the intensity of her orgasm.

Afterward, Gavin whispered in her ear, "It's so damn dark in here, and you're so quiet. I sure hope it's you I was fucking."

Karina rolled on her side and in a deep whisper, she said, "Maybe it wasn't me."

"Knock it off...that's creepy."

Her lips twitched into a smile. "What if I was actually sitting in the corner listening while you and a haggard old forest witch were making love?"

"God damn it, Karina..." He didn't care for Karina's occasionally grotesque imagination.

"I'm just playing—"

"Plus, I'd know if I was having sex with someone other than you, even in the dark," he said.

"How? Forest witches can be deceiving."

"We've been together nearly two decades. I know what you feel like...*inside* and out."

His hot breath lingered on her neck.

"But do you don't know what the inside of a haggard old forest witch feels like? Maybe it's the same."

"I imagine it would be pretty dry up in there."

"Vaginal walls like the sharp, crumbling bark of a dying tree?"

Gavin let out a laugh. "You're so nasty sometimes."

Xander's voice cut through the silence of the forest from the other tent. "I can hear you!"

Karina and Gavin snickered like a couple of teenagers sneaking through the front door past curfew. But her laughter didn't last more than a moment before the blackness of night choked it into silence.

"It's really dark out there."

"Yep."

"I have to go to the bathroom."

"Okay."

Gavin hit the solar lamp, and the tent lit up inside. He pulled a small flashlight from the hanging tent pocket and handed it to her.

Karina stood outside, looking down the hillside to the bathhouse with its single spotlight. There was nothing but pitch black between her flashlight beam and the spotlight below.

Gavin crawled out of the tent behind her.

"I gotta go, too."

"Come with me?"

She wouldn't admit she was scared to make the short walk down the hill but knew she didn't want to go alone. Her thoughts could scare the hell out of her when left alone in the dark with them.

Gavin waited outside the restroom while Karina went in. Semen dribbled out and soaked her underwear, as if it were fleeing her body. Fleeing the toxic darkness within her. Fleeing the rotting corpse of her father's ghost which stirred in her gut that night.

Inside the cinderblock restroom were two stalls and a cold-water sink. Daddy longlegs, among other pests, clung to the walls and ceiling. She used the larger, wheelchair-accessible bathroom. On the toilet, she stared at the ventilation holes at the base of the wall. Three strategically missing cinderblocks were spaced apart to allow airflow. The hole nearest her foot was more than wide enough for a snake to slither through, or a pervert attempting to steal a glimpse of her with her pants down. All she could do in that situation is stomp on his face from her seated position. A brief daydream, ornate with blood and viscera, slipped through her mind before she'd finished peeing. She couldn't tell Gavin about it, so she kept that horrific fantasy to herself.

Back in the tent, they zipped the window fearing the clouded sky might leak, and Gavin fell asleep, leaving her alone in the dark with her thoughts. She pictured a haggard old forest witch crouched in the corner of their tent, watching, breathing, waiting to climb on her husband when she finally fell asleep. But there was something more sinister watching her. The darkness became an entity of its own, looming over her like a living, breathing thing. When had it come in? There was no sound of the zipper. No rustle of tent fabric as it phased through to be near her. What if it was already in the tent with them? Maybe it was in her gut, a demonic thing, taloned hands clutched on her rib cage like prison bars. And it clawed at her insides until it broke flesh and bone and bled out, devouring any discernible light within the tent, and it moved on to eat up the light in the campground, and the world. So black she couldn't even see her hand in front of her own face no matter where she went. Before her thoughts spiraled further, she reeled them back into the confines of the tent.

Now the darkness sat on her chest, not as the haggard old witch, or some night demon, but as an imperceptible shadow figure, the liquid, nebulous thing that followed her, connected with her. Perched on her chest like a cat waiting for breakfast. Or maybe it was waiting to drown her in her sleep. Perhaps if she breathed as shallowly as possible, it wouldn't know she was there. Or perhaps her pulse, banging between her ears like a death knell, would lull it to sleep.

Night stretched its black canvas, inking out every flicker of light, and Karina thought morning would never come.

"I kept *almost* sleeping, then waking to find it was still pitch black," she said.

"I wouldn't say it was *pitch* black," Gavin said. "The bathhouse gave off some light. I could catch a bit of glow outside the tent when I woke up...like, 500 times last night."

He leaned in for a kiss. Day-old stubble made his face scratchy. A cloud of morning breath hit her. She tried not to make a sour face, at his breath, at the assault of his scruff against her skin, or at his refusal to admit how dark it was last night.

"I just laid there waiting for morning," she said. "But it just seemed to get darker and darker, like the night was sitting on my chest. Like it was going to fill up the tent with a thick, smothering oil, and drown me in my sleep."

"Wow...there's a visual."

Gavin had little patience for her many, many visuals. She wondered sometimes how she ended up with someone so utterly incompatible with her, but also so good for her.

Gavin believed, much like her mother, that sadness could be willed away with positive thinking. True for some lucky people, but for Karina, it stayed with her, always. He and others stood lofty above and often tried to shine a light into her pit of darkness, but there was always a cloud ready to obscure it.

"Anyway," Gavin said, "Nobody can drown you in black oil or anything else. Not my salty sailor."

He gave a playful punch to her shoulder and unzipped the tent. A half-dozen spiders scattered across the fabric on the outside.

She hated it when he called her that. *His salty sailor.* It was cute fifteen years ago when she was in the Navy, but she hadn't been a sailor for a long time. She wasn't the same person he'd met back then. But neither was he.

Gavin and Xander moved like cold sap in the morning, making it impossible to get out on the hiking trail early. Xander didn't talk much; he embraced his morning-zombie persona. Gavin cooked egg substitute over a butane burner. Most of them burnt, but she tried to embrace the good today. Her family was together. The hard times over the past few years created fissures between them, and the stress of everyday life made those cracks grow wider. This trip was their chance to break away from the everyday, to ease the stress on some of those fissures so the ever-widening gap between them might have a chance to narrow.

"This is nice," Karina said, folding her hands under her chin and taking in her family.

Gavin kissed her on the forehead, stubble stabbing into her skin.

"It was a good idea, dear."

She sighed. "I don't want to go back to work on Monday."

"Fuck!" Xander dropped his plastic fork on the picnic table and covered his mouth.

She'd never heard that word come from his mouth. She wasn't so naïve to believe he never said it, but certainly not in front of his parents.

Gavin stood over the eggs, spatula frozen mid-scrape.

Xander's tight-lipped expression turned foul before spitting blood onto the ground.

"Holy shit." Karina hurried to him. "What happened?"

Xander picked up the fork. "Sharp," he said through a mouthful of blood, then spat again.

She inspected the white plastic fork and found a jagged seam. The ridge of extra plastic was called *flash* in the injection-molding plastics world. As the quality control department's senior shift manager at Dathnol Plastics, Karina had rejected countless plastic parts over the last decade for the same production flaw. Sometimes, a little flash doesn't affect the quality or the effectiveness of the product, but with something like a fork, there's no way this amount of flash would pass inspection on her shift.

"Flash."

"Seriously?" Gavin took the fork and focused on the paper-thin ridge of plastic which ran along the edge of the prong. He placed his finger along its edge. "May as well have chewed on a razor blade. Holy shit!"

"There's a first aid kit in the car."

Karina signaled for Gavin to get it, then unraveled paper towels and held it out to her son. "Apply pressure."

"To my tongue?"

Blood seeped out of the corner of his mouth.

"That's a lot of blood."

Xander spat again and she pressed the paper towel wad to his face. "Take it."

He shoved it in his mouth while she checked the box of plastic forks. Every single fork had the same flaw, as she expected.

"Well, there's a lawsuit waiting to happen," she said.

After several seconds, Xander gagged and coughed out the crimson-soaked paper towels. Gavin returned with the first aid kit and unwrapped a packet of gauze.

"Where's the cut?" Gavin said. "Lemme see."

Xander spat again and tilted his head back, lifting his tongue to the roof of his mouth, exposing a gash on the underside, a razor-thin laceration, clean like a paper cut, but deep. Scarlet spilled in a deluge that pooled around his bottom teeth.

The gauze pack under the tongue helped, but after several minutes, the bleeding hadn't slowed.

"I wonder if that needs to be sutured," Karina said.

"Stitches in my tongue?"

Xander looked like a little kid again with a mouthful of cherry Kool-Aid, deep red staining his face.

"Yeah...guess we're making a quick trip to the ER today."

Gavin clapped his hands together and shut off the butane stove.

Karina sat with her son in the backseat, feeding him fresh gauze to apply under his tongue and holding a plastic bag for him to spit into. Gavin pulled up close to the ranger station and hopped out to talk to the woman inside about the nearest hospital.

While they were alone, Karina asked, "How'd you cut the *underside* of your tongue?"

Xander shrugged.

"I mean, who puts the fork *under* their tongue?"

Xander's shoulders shook, and his lips fought to hold back laughter.

Gavin's face was pinched in determination when he returned. "Okay. Twenty minutes. Hopefully you don't bleed to death before we arrive."

"You're not going to bleed to death," Karina said, rolling her eyes. "The tongue is very vascular. It looks like a lot of blood, but it's not like you severed your aorta."

Gavin turned left out of the campground and glanced back through the rearview mirror. "Why was your fork *under* your tongue, anyway?" he asked.

A mist of crimson sprayed from Xander's mouth. He covered his lips to control the laughter, but it was too late. Blood splattered across Karina's face.

She blinked ruby droplets from her eyelashes and laughter filled the car. She couldn't remember the last time they'd all laughed this hard together. Of all the things that could bring them together, she never thought it'd be blood splatter.

After wiping it from her face, she began to clean blood from the seat-backs.

"Hey, Karina..." Gavin said.

"What?"

"Did you hear Xander say *fuck*?"

He looked into the rearview mirror for a reaction.

"I did!"

Xander's lips tightened again like he was about to laugh, so she snatched his sketchbook from the seat and held it as a shield to protect her from another blood shower.

"Don't laugh!"

Xander spat into the plastic bag and snatched the sketchbook from her, joy draining from his face.

"I wasn't going to look in it," Karina said. "I know it's like your diary."

"Diary?" Gavin said.

Xander shook his head and spoke around the blood filling his mouth. "It's just a sketchbook."

His gaze turned toward the window as they rounded a sharp corner.

Her phone buzzed in her pocket, finally picking up a signal. "Where are we going? I'll map it."

"Back to that town we passed through when we came in. Right before going up the steep, mountain pass."

"What's it called?"

"Bedford."

The signal was intermittent, but after several minutes the map appeared.

"Uhh…"

Gavin's eyes found hers in the mirror.

"Bedford was the other way!"

"No. That was the town we went through!"

She checked the map. "Buchanan! We came through Buchanan. Bedford is the other direction!"

"Shit…two B towns. Okay! Okay!" Gavin threw his hands in the air, and for that moment she worried he'd lose control of the vehicle.

She took a deep breath and fought the waves of negativity, but their son was bleeding and Gavin took the fucking *wrong turn!* She zoomed out and searched for a closer hospital. "There's a one in Roanoke. I don't like the idea of turning around on these narrow roads, anyway."

"Got it…" Gavin sighed. "Sorry, I thought—"

"It's okay." It wasn't okay, but she didn't want to argue. She wished she could live forever in that ephemeral moment of joy in the woods with her family. How silly of her to think being somewhere different would change anything.

Xander's face drooped as if auditioning for a role of angsty teen. To anyone else, he'd look emotionless. But she knew there was something inside his head, other than pooling blood, filling him with darkness, like her and her father. Maybe there was no hope for him to ever be happy.

The horrible thoughts pressed against bone from the inside. They tested the integrity of her skull, aching to get out of her head. Karina closed her eyes and tried to let some light into her soul. She had a healthy, happy family…

*…but do you really?*

Gavin started the steep descent down the mountain, taking each switchback with a careful approach, old brakes squealing in protest. She appreciated his thoughtfulness. Any other day, he might've taken the road faster to get a rise out of her. But he knew her stress levels were already at maximum capacity. She reached forward and placed a hand on his shoulder. He smiled in the mirror and returned his eyes to the road.

"We'll be there soon," she said to Xander, patting her other hand on his knee.

No matter what terrible things entered her mind, these were her people. Her life. She needed to let them in. No matter how dark it got, they would always have to be her light. They had to be. Because there was nothing else without them.

The Accord rolled faster downhill, coming to another sharp turn. Gavin's fists clenched at ten and two o'clock. Rough, aging skin stretched thin over mountainous knuckles. He didn't say anything, but she leaned to check the steadily climbing speedometer, and to see his right foot pressed to the floor on the brake pedal. The pedal hissed as he removed his foot and pressed again. By the time she looked back to the road their vehicle had burst through the roadside brush and flew off the side of the mountain. Unbuckled, as she'd been too distracted tending to Xander, she lifted off her seat. The contents of her purse and yesterday's coffee cups suspended mid-air. Karina braced for impact.

Fluorescent lights assaulted her eyes. A pulsing beep of a monitor. The odor of disinfectant. She knew she was in a hospital but couldn't remember why. Did she have a surgery scheduled? She'd been talking about getting her tubes tied for years...

Her right forearm ached. Something was wrapped around it. A cast.

The memory cut through the pain and the fog of waking. The car landed, bottomed out on a rocky outcrop. She'd smacked into the seat and curled into a ball on the floor. One hand on Xander's leg; he was buckled in. The painted image of their dead faces in reds and fleshy pinks flashed before her, and that was all she could remember.

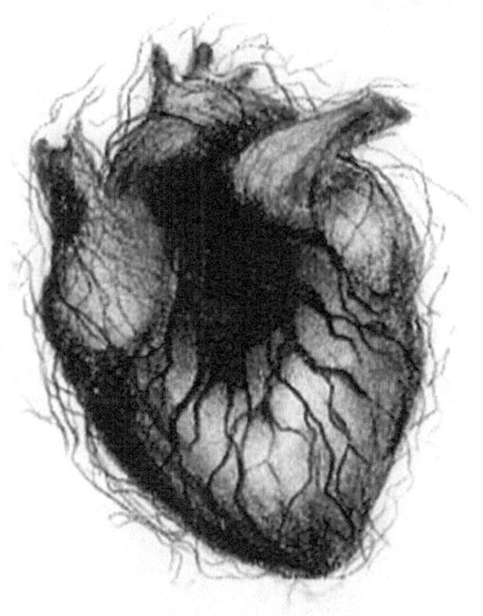

# Chapter 3

Funerals are a strange ceremony. Why are there so many cut flowers? Why, to honor the lives of those we loved, do we slice through the stems of roses and tulips and lilies, cutting short the lives of something else? Why do we watch as their bodies are lowered into the ground, escorted by slowly dying flowers give their last display of beauty? And why do we trust a stranger in a robe to tell us what will happen with their soul?

As the robed man with a Bible spoke of God's will, Karina felt nothing. She stared at two caskets. The bodies inside had been doctored by an artist of the dead. Brain matter and blood cleaned away and painted over. Skull patched with latex or caulk or chicken wire and plaster, or whatever they use to reconstruct the face to insulate those who come to pay their respects from reality. Why not leave the dead with their injuries? With their bulging eye sockets and ruptured organs? Why not show the world the severed spinal cords and mangled faces exhibiting the horrors of their loved one's final moments? Why cover it up and pretend there was anything peaceful about their graphic and violent deaths?

The funeral director's voice droned on and Karina drifted. The distance between her and her family became so immeasurable over the years. Now, there'd be a velvet lining, a solid oak box, and six feet of compacted soil to separate them. How would their bodies decompose over time? How long would it take before the wood's varnish wore off? Before the rainwater seeped deep enough into the earth to dribble into the casket? Before the worms burrowed between the weakening wood structure of the casket and began to feed?

Her body ached in the graveside aluminum chair. Trembling palms squeezed her temples, fighting the pressure building within, but she couldn't contain it. Tears spilled onto the grass between her feet.

Her mother's hand landed feather-soft on her back. Helen well knew the pain of losing a husband, but Karina didn't want her touch. Nor did she want her mother's love, not anymore. Each year, the poison in her words became more potent, more lethal. Karina squirmed beneath her mother's hand and straightened her back. Tears continued to fall, but she clenched her jaw and fought like hell to stop the flow. More than anything she wanted to sit alone in the darkness.

Grief is a monster. A world-wrecking monster that ravages the body and mind and spirit. Fighting back feels like the only way to manage the attack. Some people fight back with anger, some with prayer. Some with a mask of optimism. Karina believed she deserved her grief. That she deserved the monster's unrelenting blows. Absorb the pain and bottle it up deep within; live with it. Let the demon rattle at her rib cage, snarling and hungry. Let it devour her slowly from the inside out. Maybe she wasn't allowed to get angry and lash out because she'd brought this on herself. Her family was dead because she, deep down in that sick, subconscious mind, had willed it to happen.

What follows the funeral is worse regarding ridiculous traditions. Food. So much food. Family and friends unseen for years crawl out of the cracks and crevices of our lives like cockroaches. Karina didn't believe they were here for the food, but rather to check a box showing they cared. Many of the people here had gathered last year at Mom's house after Dad died. Like a damn family reunion, but the family was dwindling away. At least the family that mattered. This gathering was much bigger than Dad's. Gavin had met and made friends with a lot of people over his twenty years in the Navy. Dad was more of a recluse, an artist who worked quietly alone most of his life.

Karina managed to slip away from the gatherers taking up space in the open-concept kitchen and living room. She escaped to the screened porch where her old shipmate, Clara, stood chatting with Mom, fluffing the cushions on the outdoor sofa.

She walked in as Clara said, "Helen, sit down. You've done enough."

Mom feigned exhaustion and some sense of being overwhelmed and sat gently on the sofa. Her silver-blonde hair had thinned, but she kept it styled in a way to cover the patches where scalp was visible. Mom liked to cover up all the things she thought were unbecoming of perfection. Karina lowered herself into the wicker chair that she and Gavin had bought at a yard sale years ago.

Mom brushed some invisible stray fiber from Karina's shoulder. "If I knew you needed a new black wardrobe, I could've gone shopping for you."

Clara swooped in to save Karina the trouble of fighting with her mom, "I don't think picking an outfit was on her mind."

Clara was always the stylish one. Never following the trends, but creating her own. Today, she wore flared black pants and a black shirt with billowing sleeves. Sashes around her waist and across her forehead. It was as if Valentino or Chanel dressed a pirate for the Oscars. Today her hair was braided. Dozens of thin braids, tied back loosely into a bunch at the nape of her neck. Her hairstyles changed often over the years, from slick black locks, to a natural afro, from loose shoulder-length curls to high-top fades and buzzcuts and pixie cuts.

"The braids are nice," Karina said. "I haven't seen you in braids in a long time."

Clara nodded, tight-lipped at first, but she was never one to hold back her thoughts. "I've had braids for three years now."

"Oh…" A little twinge of guilt jabbed at Karina, but it didn't add much to the already blackening wound within her. It'd been hard to keep up with friends and family over the years. Life had a way of getting away from her.

Helen shook her head and smiled at Clara. "My Karina was never good about keeping up with relationships."

She hoped her mother would refrain from the usual critiques considering the circumstances. Even at a funeral, Mom could not resist pointing out her shortcomings. This jab about keeping up with relationships felt like a poker straight from the fire.

Mom blamed Karina for not visiting enough. She said Karina was selfish, that she was stubborn. Mom would say anything if it meant she didn't have to face the reality; as the years progressed, it was Dad who pulled away from the family. He was the one who didn't show up when Karina needed him. He was the one who retreated to other rooms when she visited with Xander, his only grandson.

"But…" Mom patted Clara on the knee. "…she visited Dale more often after his stroke, so I appreciate that."

Mom dabbed a handkerchief under her dry eyes.

Karina would've liked to tear into her mother, but she had no energy to fight. In the corner of her eye, where she thought she felt a burning sensation of tears trying to form, a dark spot clouded her vision. She wiped, but realized it wasn't in her eyes. A patch of missing light was in her periphery. A darkness taking the form of a silhouetted person. She turned to see who stood in the corner of the porch where Gavin left a few of his woodworking tools, but there was nothing. Nothing but the half-finished chainsaw carving of a bear. He bought all the tools, various saws, chisels, and even a custom-made branding iron with a logo of an anchor. Gavin had taken up the hobby of woodcutting shortly after his Navy retirement. The faceless bear wasn't more than an abstract carving of wood to anyone else, but Karina knew what Gavin had intended for it to be.

The screened porch allowed in a damp, cool air. The earthy wet smell of spring. Tulips around the oak tree out back offered a splash of color against the dull grass.

"I'm sorry," Clara broke the silence. "I don't know what to say in situations like this. But I want you to know that I'm here if you need anything..."

Karina nodded. Clara had been her best friend on the ship until Gavin. They stayed friends for a long time. Every few months, they'd meet for drinks or see a band. But those visits grew further apart. Karina kept finding excuses not to visit. She wasn't sure why, other than it was a lot of work to maintain the friendship. Work, family, and all the obligations that come with owning a home took priority in her life and there was little room for anything else.

Mom smiled. "That's why I adore you, Clara. You're a good, thoughtful person."

Clara closed her eyes and bowed with her hands pressed together to accept the compliment humbly.

"And..." Mom's smile grew. "You are simply luminous! Look at your face. It just glows with positivity."

"All right, Helen, that's enough praise for one day." Clara stood waving airily with a smile. She placed a hand on Karina's shoulder. "Need a drink?"

Karina nodded.

"I got you, girl." She opened the door to the house and left Karina alone with her mother on the porch.

"Karina, dear..." Helen stood to adjust the pile of shoes by the door. Most of them were Gavin's and Xander's. "What are you going to do now?"

Karina scanned her mother's face looking for some sign of what she was getting at.

Mom stood up straight and sighed. "I only mean, are you staying here?"

"Why wouldn't I?"

"I don't know, you always talked about living in the mountains."

"Well, yeah. But I haven't thought about that yet."

"Really?" Mom's eyebrows climbed up her forehead with disbelief.

"What's that supposed to mean?"

"Only that you've wanted to live in the mountains since you were a little girl, but Gavin's job kept you on the coast."

"Gavin retired and we could've moved, but—"

"You were working too, I know. And now you'll have his life insurance."

"Jesus, Mom, can we let the fucking dirt settle first?"

Fury clawed within, it lacerated the walls of her chest cavity and wanted to climb up her throat and unleash.

She held her palms up in surrender. "I just figured you already had a plan."

Mom held her gaze as if she thought she knew some deep dark secret, the way a private investigator in a bad movie might let the bad guy know they're onto them.

"No. I don't have a plan yet, Mom."

"Considering your history..." Mom stood and paced the porch, pinching her lips together in a straight line. "Well, I don't know how to say it."

Karina stood to meet her face to face. "Just say it."

Mom leaned in and whispered, "Don't pretend you didn't want this to happen. I know, somehow, you did this."

# Chapter 4

Clara returned with a vodka tonic, head turning from Karina to Helen.

Karina's heart may as well have been made of cement, the way it fell to her gut at her mother's words. Blood drained from her face and her extremities, but she steadied her fear and fury and took the drink from Clara using her left hand. It was difficult getting used to using her non-dominant hand while the hairline fracture in her forearm healed.

Helen fluttered her eyelashes beneath eyebrows that could not arch any higher in self-righteousness, and she went inside, leaving Karina and Clara on the porch.

"That seemed tense. Y'all good?" Clara asked.

Karina swigged from the mostly-vodka tonic. "Good ol' Helen Marsh blames me for the death of my family, that's all."

"Jesus fucking Christ."

Clara sipped from a teacup.

"No drink for you?"

Clara held her chin up. "I quit two years ago."

Karina tried to smile, she felt it wanting to grace her face, but it manifested as no more than a twitch to one corner of her mouth. "How do you feel?"

"I feel good. I'm healthy. I feel...clear for once."

"Good."

Clara's face went sour. "But seriously, what the fuck is with your mother?"

"She thinks I made it happen. She thinks everything bad that ever happens in her life is because of me."

"Fuck. Why would—"

"When I was a little girl, I saw a movie about a home invasion—"

"Ah," Clara interrupted, nodding with a smirk. "Home Alone, eh?"

Karina appreciated the effort to make a joke, but there was no place for joy right now. She continued, "No. I don't remember the name of it. But I was so scared. I was obsessed.

I thought about it for months, wondering if it'd ever happen to us. I envisioned all the scenarios of people breaking in with guns and bombs. I imagined getting held captive and zip-tied to a chair. I even imagined fighting them off with Mom's cast iron frying pan."

"Those are some elaborate daydreams."

"I've always had them, since as long as I can remember. Mom hated it."

"Kids daydream and play make-believe."

"And then one day it actually happened. They came in while my mom and I were making cookies. They held a gun on us. There were two of them. They argued for a moment, then grabbed Mom's purse, and the CD player and a few other things. Whatever was within reach."

Clara's jaw hung open for a moment before saying, "Sounds like a smash and grab, but they didn't expect you all to be home."

"Exactly. We were fine. But later that night, I told my mom that I'd daydreamed it. That I knew it would happen to us one day."

"And she freaked?"

"No. Not that time. She said it was a weird coincidence."

Clara squinted, trying to make sense of where Karina was going with the story.

"Then it happened again in high school. I kept thinking Mom and Dad would break up. So many kids at school had divorced parents. It was weird that mine were still together. I just kept daydreaming about them breaking up. Eventually, Dad left. Only for a few months, but he was gone."

"Just like that? Or were they arguing for a while first?"

"I heard them arguing all the time."

Clara set her tea on the table. "It was going to happen whether you thought about it or not."

"Explain that to my mother..."

"So what? She thinks you wished your family to..."

Karina nodded.

"Did you?"

The question caught her off-guard, but she held her breath, still and stoic, hoping not to show a reaction.

"I'm sorry," Clara said. "I don't mean it as an accusation. I mean it more out of curiosity. Did you daydream about losing your family? It's not bad if you did. People worry about that stuff all the time."

"I worried I'd lose them. All the time." Tears burned under her eyelids.

"Everybody worries about losing their loved ones. That doesn't mean you made it happen. That is, unless something very specific happened, then how can you even think for a second your daydreaming is connected?"

The cement heart inched its way up into her throat, refusing to let her divulge her secret. She swallowed it and shook her head. "No. It wasn't anything specific."

She sat on the sofa in the living room while visitors from various commands throughout Gavin's career chatted and cracked jokes, cracked beers. Neighbors and teachers reminisced about Xander being "so quiet, but a good kid." A thick fog filled the house, a viscous substance through which people passed, voices muffled, condolences shrouded in the haze of Karina's despair.

Slowly, Karina's home emptied. Friends and family trickled out, and only Mom and Clara remained. Karina hadn't moved from the couch in over an hour. She wasn't sure if she ever would. She closed her eyes for what seemed like a moment, but when she opened them, a blanket lay across her chest and Mom and Clara stood in the kitchen, wrapping casserole dishes and running the dishwasher.

"You don't have to do that," Karina said, but they *did* have to do it. She didn't have an ounce of strength within her to wash a dish, to wipe down a counter, or take out garbage. As well, any chore was made more complex by the broken state of her arm.

"Don't be stupid." Clara adjusted a sash around her waist.

Mom sat beside Karina on the sofa. The cushions sank and Karina had to lean the opposite way so as not to fall into her mom. Helen's arm wrapped around her daughter's back. "I know what this feels like Kare-bear."

That was the name her dad had given her when she was a little girl, and he rarely used it as she got older. But it was a name Helen never used. Karina pulled away from her mother's toxic touch.

There was a time she was a good mom. Bedtime stories, healthy snacks and notes in her lunch box. Homework help and prom dress shopping. Though Helen had been a bit of a discount Martha Stewart on the surface, and always conscious of appearances, she was a good mom. In many ways, Karina was closer to her mother through her teenage years, back when Dad had struggled with *the darkness*, as Mom so liked to call it.

After her parents split, temporarily, Mom leaned into her suspicions. Karina daydreamed them into marital destruction and Mom wasn't afraid to randomly say so over the years.

After Dad's stroke, Helen changed for the worse. She controlled every aspect of his life because he could no longer speak for himself. Hell, he could barely hold a fork. She dressed him in a blue and orange reflective tracksuit nearly every day. She'd found the outfit on sale and bought three sets because the elastic band pants made it easier to help him in the bathroom. His paintbrushes became defiant of his grip, and even when Karina brought Xander over to help his grandfather hold it, Mom shooed them out of the house because Dad was "too tired to paint today." He lost the ability to do all the things he loved and became a prisoner in his mind. Mom held the key.

The moment Mom became the puppeteer of his life, a wall went up inside her. The nicer mom Karina remembered from her childhood was trapped behind an impenetrable barrier, even when Karina needed her the most.

"I'm going to bed now," Karina said. The clock on the stove read 7 pm.

She ushered Mom out the door, picturing her heading home on the highway at night, 45 minutes away in Windsor. Her night vision wasn't great and her vision in general worsened in her 60s. Karina wondered what it was like to return to an empty house. No music from a teenager's room. No life partner or best friend to greet you. Not even a cat to rub against your leg. Karina had been staying at her mom's house since the accident and had yet to spend the night alone in her own home.

Karina understood why Mom had become so bitter and spiteful. She took her frustration out on her daughter, on the only person in the world who would absorb the blows and not fight back.

"Are you okay?" Clara asked from behind the kitchen island.

Karina closed the front door and felt pulled to the couch like water circling a drain.

"That was a stupid question. I mean, you and your mom…"

Karina felt herself nodding, but she was so weak it was likely imperceptible from Clara's point of view.

Down the hall, a light was on in the bathroom, swaths of shadows between her and it. Empty bedrooms awaited her, but she couldn't stand the thought of traversing that impossibly difficult path to nothingness.

Karina noticed a figure out of the corner of her eye. A lingering party guest? It stood to the left of Clara. When she looked straight-on, though, there was nothing. Just a trick of the light and a ragged mind eager to find meaning in shadows. She rubbed palms into her eyelids to relieve the itchiness of her dry eyes.

"I keep seeing spots in the corner of my eyes. Like dark patches. Shadows where there aren't shadows," Karina said, squinting. "Maybe I should get my eyes checked."

"Probably those vitreous floater things. They're super common, but you should definitely get that checked out just in case."

"In case what?"

"I'm not playing WebMD and telling you might have cancer. Because you don't. Just take some time for yourself and then make an appointment. I'm sure it's nothing serious."

Though vitreous floaters made sense, something felt wrong. It wasn't a speck in the corner of her eye. It had form. Human, or upright animal, and she'd seen it in the woods, behind trees on the mountain. She felt its presence in her tent. The only other thing that made sense was that she'd been hallucinating, and she wasn't ready to face that potential reality.

"Do you want me to stay tonight?" Clara asked.

"No. You should go home. Are you still with...uh..." *The bleach blonde goth? What was her name?* "Valerie?"

"God, no. I've been dating a guy named Brent for almost a year." She pointed a finger. "You and I have a lot of catching up to do. For Christ's sake I've been working right over in Norfolk for over a year now."

"I'm sorry I never came to see the store."

"Well, you've never really been interested in what my shop has to offer."

"Who knew there were so many witches and psychics in the Hampton Roads area?" Karina attempted what should have been normal conversation, but it felt like speaking an otherworldly language she hadn't fully learned. The effort to be social was exhausting.

"Crystals, incense, Ouija boards, and tarot. People, even normies like you, eat that shit up. Even if it's not your thing, you should come out next week. I'll show you around Onyx Oracle and Oddities...also known as *OOO*." She waggled her fingers like a plotting witch.

"I will," Karina said, unsure if that was the truth.

"Will you be okay tonight?"

Karina nodded.

"I have some edibles if you want to take the edge off. They're pretty chill and should help you sleep."

"I haven't had an edible since...I don't know when. With Gavin in the military, you know."

"You couldn't. But now it's legal, so here." She pulled out a vial and shook two out into her hand. "Start with half. Fuck it. In your state, have a whole tablet. You need to sleep."

The edible kicked in and for the first time in days, the muscles in her shoulders relaxed. Maybe sleep was possible this evening. She headed into the dark hallway, her body floating through the palpable night. Nerve endings in her skin were at attention, noting every molecule of air on her flesh. Goosebumps rose on her arms as she neared her son's bedroom. She stepped inside but didn't feel welcome. This space had been closed to her for a couple of years now. The only time she was permitted inside was when Xander was in school, and she'd pop in to grab some laundry or dirty dishes.

Xander's walls were not adorned with band posters like many teenagers but with prints of artwork he liked. Some of that art was painted by her father, Dale. Horror art. Monsters and gnashing teeth. Winged demons and serpents. Xander's art reminded her of her father's. She wished she knew what had happened to his sketchbook after the accident because it wasn't in the box of things returned to her.

She sat on his bed, springs creaking, and she crumpled into a fetal ball. Head on his pillow, breathing in the sweaty stench he'd left behind. If only she were more... or less... He could've grown up to be... The darkness within squeezed. It invaded every cell of her being, filled her with a black despair and swelled until each molecule within needed to burst. It pressed so hard, and she tried to keep the pain bottled up tight within the mold of her grieving frame, but it couldn't be contained. She burst into tears, bleeding them out onto Xander's pillow. The room filled with a weight she couldn't bear, and she wished she'd die from the pain rather than suffer another moment alive.

Karina woke in the middle of the night to see a figure standing by the bed. It was a silhouette, almost formless, but she could make out the shape of a head and shoulders. When she realized a person loomed so closely, she jolted upright, pressing herself against the wall.

It remained. Her eyes tried to focus, but the nebulous thing did not have a solid shape. Something primal rose within her and climbed from her gut, up her throat and released in a scream. She kicked away and scrambled off the foot of the bed to flip on the light.

When the corner lamp lit the room, the shadowy thing didn't disappear. It lingered in the shape and size of a grown man who'd been covered with a sheet made of the darkest storm clouds. The shadow lightened, but never moved, eventually dissipating into nothingness.

# CHAPTER 5

"No more edibles," Karina told Clara in the morning.

"They don't make you hallucinate. Are you sure there wasn't someone in your house? Jesus, Karina, you should've called the police."

"And tell them what? I saw a...a shadow?"

Clara was quiet on the other end. "I guess not. But if you were hallucinating, I highly doubt it was from the edible. Maybe you need to talk to someone. A psychologist or something?"

"I don't like talking to people."

"I know. But you've lost so much. You can't keep all that inside."

Clara and Mom popped in to visit several times over the next few days. The emptiness of her house was tangible. A void that constricted, choked, slinked into her periphery as a silhouetted sheet-man. Perhaps she should've taken Clara's advice about talking to a psychologist, but she couldn't manage to make the phone call. To ask for help. She didn't deserve help after what she'd done to her family. No. She'd rather bear the insufferable laceration to her sanity. She deserved to be judged by the dark spirit, allow it to hold a blade to her wrist, deep enough to hurt, to leave a scar so she would remember, always.

Her guilty conscience welcomed the torture.

Mom's visits, however, were unwelcome, but Karina let her in anyway. She mostly helped with chores since Karina's arm would be in a cast for a few weeks. Mom entertained with the façade of being a helpful, consoling mother, but the resentful and judgmental woman within found its way out.

"Do you really think this is my fault?" Karina held a warm coffee mug to her lips but set it down because she couldn't stomach the thought of enjoying it.

There was no immediate denial. She showed no remorse for the accusations made earlier in the week. Instead, Mom set down her coffee and tilted her head. "Not directly, of course."

The words rushed over her as a wave of betrayal.

Mom continued, "You have the darkness, just like your father."

"Most people call it depression, Mom."

Her eyelids fluttered shut, and she shook her head. "Whatever you want to call it, doesn't matter. You have a sadness. When you combine that with a sick imagination..."

"It's just—"

Mom held up her hand. "You think the most terrible things. And those things you daydream about. You and I both *know* that they have a way of coming true."

"That's not even possible." Karina pushed away from the table, wanting to yell, wanting to fight. She took a calming breath. "If I could daydream things into existence, I'd be a millionaire by now. Do you know how many times I dreamed of winning the lottery? How many hours I've spent caught in my own head, wondering what I'd do with the money? I dreamed it so many times, more than I've daydreamed about anything else. And guess what? I never won the lottery, did I?"

Mom eyed her coffee and she leaned back in her chair, crossing her arms. "You don't have to get angry with me."

An inclination toward violence bubbled within. Karina imagined another person would've kicked their mother out of their life. They would've thrown a punch or spewed hateful profanities. But Karina absorbed the blows, yet again.

"I'm trying to help you, Karina. I'm trying to guide you through the pain, to keep you from continuing down a path to *more* destruction."

Karina's eye twitched. A subtle spasm in her lower lid, like there was a tiny little demon inside wanting to jump out and devour her mother. "What more destruction could I possibly cause?" Instead of a demon, tears brimmed. "I've lost everything."

Mom nodded. "Why don't you come with me to church on Sunday? My pastor would love to meet you. She might be able to help with all this."

Karina used the edge of her sleeve to absorb the tears before they dribbled out. She sniffled up the leak in her nose and toughened her exterior. "Unless she can bring back Gavin and Xander, then she can't help me."

"Don't talk like that. That's the kind of sick stuff I mean. You get yourself into these situations because you're sick."

Karina's jaw clenched around words of cruelty. Her fingers folded into bricks. "I have an overactive imagination. That's all. That's the way I've always been. It doesn't mean anything."

Mom turned her back to Karina and moved to the kitchen window over the sink. "You used to tell the most grotesque stories when you were a little girl. You remember that?"

Karina abandoned any attempt at a rational conversation with her mother, and instead breathed through the fury.

"My goodness, you were in the fourth grade, I believe, when your teacher showed me a story you wrote about a monster who ate elbows."

A grin sparked on her face, remembering the elbow-eating monster. She'd almost forgotten.

Mom twisted around and crossed her arms. "It was disturbing."

"I was a kid!"

"It was very graphic. Blood and, well, I don't even remember, but it was a terrible, dark thing for a little girl to write. I worried you'd dive into that darkness and become just like your father."

"Dad was a well-respected artist, Mom!"

"Well respected by whom, though? A bunch of degenerates who gobble up gore and disgusting stories! I loved your father, but his art was sick. Just like him."

"It was *just art*!"

"Was it though? Or was it something more?"

Any remaining respect for her mother evaporated.

"Let me help you, Kare."

"Don't call me that." Her voice raised, cracked as the fissure between her mother and herself widened.

"I'm sorry," Mom said. "But please. The investigation of the car's brake system didn't turn up anything that should've caused that accident."

"The brake pads were bad. I told them that."

Mom waved dismissively. "I simply want to make sure nothing else bad happens."

"How about this?" Karina said, defeated. "I'll imagine up something positive. Will that make you happy?" Karina closed her eyes and put her hands together in a mock prayer.

"Xander, sitting right here next to me. I'll undo everything, and look! There's Gavin, too. And even better, *you're* not here." Karina opened her eyes to lock her gaze on her mother.

Nothing could calm the raging storm within. Nothing to mend the damage caused by Mom's cavalier accusations. Knifed in the belly, gutted and left on the slaughterhouse floor. The blade stirred around with the ghosts and rotting corpses of her child, her husband, and her father. Their bodies filling her up with decay and regret. Karina would carry the weight of their deaths for eternity so she wouldn't be alone in the dark.

More days passed and Helen hadn't visited, but the shadow thing made several appearances. She preferred it to seeing her mother. Whether it was real, or some conjured hallucination didn't matter.

It materialized when she woke in the night. It stood outside the shower curtain, silhouetted against steamy light. It crept into the doorways and watched her sleep. She feared if she didn't find out what it was, or what it wanted, if anything, it'd never leave her alone.

Last night, it lurked near the coat rack when her neighbor Wendel stopped by with a pan of lasagna from the grocery deli.

"I picked it up ten minutes ago, so it's still hot," he said, offering to carry the piping hot foil pan inside to her kitchen with the potholders rather than pass it off to her. Wendel set the pan on the counter. "Are you hungry?" He peeled back the foil lid and a waft of sauce and noodles tempted her. Her stomach cramped with the desire to be filled with something other than emptiness.

"Not right now, but thank you. Maybe for dinner, later."

"It's dinner time now." Wendel nodded to the clock which read 6 pm.

Time is a blurry thing when grief has filled a person. "I'm not that hungry lately, you know."

Wendel glided in like a hawk and placed a talon on her shoulder. His breath and body too close. Karina pulled back, and he allowed her some space, but his intentions were clear. There were too many barbecues and gatherings where he'd manage to get Karina alone and joke about her leaving her husband for him.

*Trade him in for a premium model.* Cringe-worthy flirtations she'd never taken very seriously. Until last night.

Wendel had taken both her hands into his. Karina didn't hide the furrow in her brow, or her lip curling in disgust. His thumbs caressed her skin, and he told her he would be there for her if she needed *anything*.

A tall shadow formed behind him. She turned around to see if someone had entered the room, but it was only the two of them in her kitchen. He said something about her being *lonely*, but she lost focus on words and could only see the cloud of black right behind his frame.

Like time had been lately, the interaction was a blur and she shoved him out the door with a placid *thank you* before the darkness decided to swallow him whole.

That night, while she lay in her bed, the shadow thing stood in the doorway watching her, waiting. Her heart was a solid lump of dead flesh in her torso. It couldn't beat. It couldn't do anything when the shadow thing was around. So, she closed her eyes and wished it would leave her alone. She wished her mother would never come by the house again. And she wished Gavin and Xander would come back to her.

Wendel had gone home alone that evening, and she imagined that he had a lot to think about. Hitting on a widow before the dirt settled over her husband's corpse. She thought of him sitting home alone, shameful and kicking himself. She pictured him in his house, drinking himself silly until he couldn't bear the weight of the humiliation. Wendel said that he understood loneliness, probably because he also carries a darkness. His depression and despair and stupidity would be too much to take, and Wendel would fix up a rope and hang himself. Relieve the world of his existence...

But before she could let the daydream take over, Karina shoved it out and sought light in the darkness. Positivity.

She focused on Xander and Gavin, dreaming of a life together in the mountains. It would be a quaint cabin in the wilderness. They wouldn't have to worry about money because Gavin's life insurance policy would hold her over. The intrusion of his death made her vision of them disappear, and she was left alone in the woods with nothing but long spindly shadows from the trees forming prison bars.

Karina broke away from the dream. She may as well have been a ghost herself, floating aimlessly through the house. After deciding to call it a night, she hovered over the porcelain sink in the bathroom to wash her face. Eyes closed as she splashed away the soap. She felt something enter the room. It was a thick, solid presence. The feeling of someone over her shoulder. Historically, when this feeling presented, she would slowly turn around, or sometimes spin as quickly as possible, to find there was absolutely nothing there. But that night, she knew it wouldn't be the case. She blotted her dripping face with a hand towel and lifted her head, eyes closed, facing the mirror. When she opened them, Xander was in the mirror behind her. His face was slick with crimson, mouth spilling blood like a dribbling brook. His eyes were not lifelessly bored, but rather bulging from the impact. The unforgiving seat-back had crushed his skull and pressurized his eyeballs out of his sockets. The image was one buried deep in her subconscious mind. Trauma had allowed her to forget, but it came back as Xander stood behind her.

Karina whipped around to see her boy, to hold him, but in the brief second required to make the turn, he vanished. She reached for the space he'd occupied, but there was nothing. No cold spot. No warmth. No sweaty smell of his head. All that existed of him was a static charge like the feeling right before a storm. It dissipated to nothingness as quickly as his visual form had retreated.

"Xander?" Arms outstretched, she fumbled for him through the air. "Xander?" She tried turning her back to the sink and closing her eyes. Retracing the steps of washing her face and looking into the mirror, but the ritual failed.

"Please come back," she said, voice breaking even at a whisper. Saliva bubbling to the surface of her lips. She wiped away her drool and tears. "What are you trying to tell me? What can I do to help? What can I do to bring you back to me?"

When she posed the question aloud, it occurred to her that, despite her denial, she did have the ability to make things happen. If she could figure out how, Karina could *will* her son back into existence.

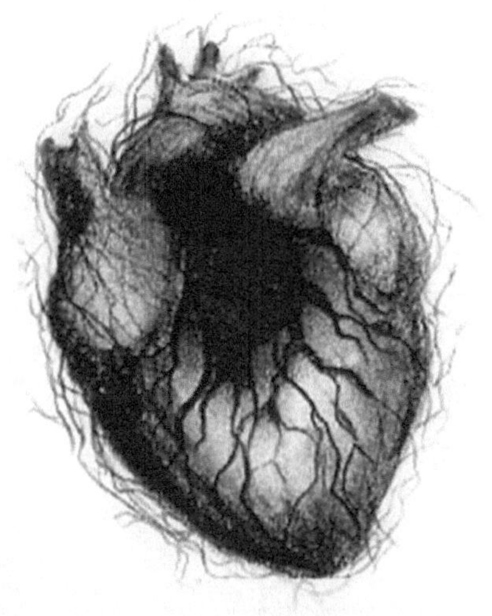

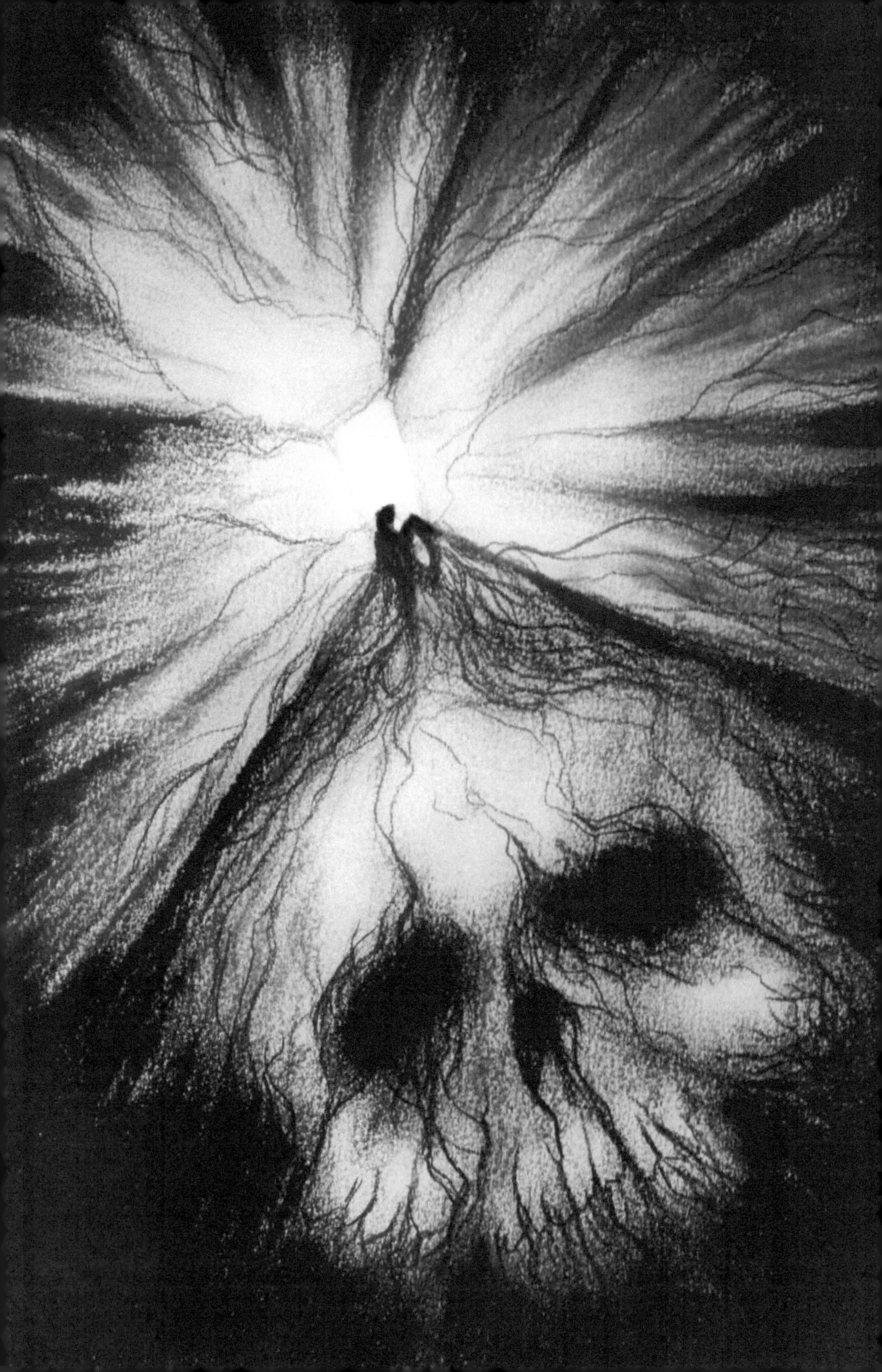

# CHAPTER 6

All night, she warred against sleep so she could dream about bringing them back. Her old fantasies of winning the lottery and buying a mountain home gave way to a simple desire: having her family back. She thought about them walking through the door in the morning, ragged and rough, but alive. They'd simply gotten lost in the wilderness after the accident. She must've imagined the scenario in eighty different ways that night, but by morning, her house was just as empty as the night before. Nothing occupied the space but herself and the shadow.

Its unrelenting presence lurked around corners and in doorways. It taunted, nagged her to *do* something, but she didn't know what it wanted.

"I see you," she whispered at first, but it didn't move. It didn't make a sound.

"I don't know what you want." As she spoke to the shadow figure, hallucination, ghost, or whatever it was, she felt a subtle snap in her head. An imperceptible hairline crack, similar to the one in her arm, had formed in her brain. The more she entertained this idea that her hallucinations of her dead son, of the dark shadow were real—*they had to be hallucinations, right?* —the more that crack would widen, and she'd fall into the oblivion of insanity.

It was time to admit she needed help.

Karina made her first visit to Clara's store, Onyx Oracle and Oddities, in Norfolk. As she climbed the stairs to the second-floor location, the aroma of herbs and incense grew stronger. Sunlight poured through large storefront windows. Neatly organized boxes of crystals and clumps of sage. Books and tarot decks and porcupine quills.

"You finally made it," Clara said as a tinkling bell accompanied her entrance.

Karina crossed her arms, eyes dry and in need of rest. She didn't realize until this moment that she hadn't even brushed her hair or reapplied deodorant. "There's something wrong with me."

"There's nothing wrong with you." Clara rolled her eyes and set down a folder. "Other than the fact that you're grieving."

"I don't know what to do."

"I told you to talk to someone!" Clara said, more anger than concern in her voice.

"I don't like talking about my feelings," Karina said.

"Nobody does. But you have to do it. Especially now."

A gaunt, pale person stalked by carrying a box. Their red hair was short and slicked back behind their ears. A flat chest, soft facial features. They were so fair skinned, Karina wondered how they avoided the sunlight lancing through the windows. A name tag was pinned on a loose cotton top that looked like it was hand woven during Biblical times.

Clara nodded. "Van, this is Karina."

Van glanced up from the box they held, but did not acknowledge Karina. There was a ghostliness to their presence, a disconnect from the world in front of their eyes. Where do you want the new shipment of oracle cards?"

Clara shrugged. "Wherever..."

Van slid a blade from their pocket and worked on opening the box.

"Van works here," Clara said, noting the strange look that must've been obvious on Karina's face. "They come from a long family history of mediums and people in touch with the other side of nature, you know?"

"The other side of nature?"

Clara shrugged. She'd always been more of an agnostic when it came to the belief in the supernatural. But she believed enough to open an oracle shop. Or maybe she simply believed enough in the money-making potential of the wealthier area of her store location.

"If you're not going to talk to a psychologist, talk to *someone*." Clara straightened some small display boxes on the counter.

"I'm talking to *you*," Karina said.

"No way. Nope. I'm not the equivalent of a shrink. You lost your family and the first day I saw you, I put a drink in your hand. That's not the kind of advice you need."

Karina moved around to the other side of the counter and sat in a cushioned chair against the wall. "I'm seeing things," she said.

The store quieted. Van's eyes subtly twitched from the box they'd been unpacking.

Clara stopped and turned, giving Karina her full attention. "What kind of things?"

"I saw Xander."

"Jesus Christ, Kare..." Clara looked to the ceiling with her hands on her hips.

"I know."

"I want to make you an appoint—"

"What'd Xander look like?" Van demanded.

Karina's lip twitched, unsure how to respond. "What the hell kind of question is that?"

Van was unfazed by Karina's hostility. There was a curiosity in their tortured eyes, and in some way, Karina knew from the gentle approach, they were only trying to help.

She released a breath and decided to tell them what had been happening. She described the nebulous dark shadow and its incessant presence.

Van spoke with a calm and quiet demeanor. They spoke humbly, but confidently in the knowledge they had to share. "And you believe this is your son?"

"I don't know what to believe. I kept seeing it. By my bed. In the hallway. It was standing right next to you a few nights ago when you were done doing the dishes." Karina made eye contact with Clara, whose mouth opened, but no words came out.

Clara shivered. "Why didn't you tell me?"

"I thought I was seeing things. Like dark spots."

"The vitreous floaters..." Clara recalled.

"And then I saw Xander. Not the cloudy black smudge, but *Xander*."

"What did he look like?" Van asked again.

Karina held tight to the image of his bloodied face, refusing to share the image she'd seen. Not the bulging eyeballs. Not the blood spilling from his mouth. "He looked like my kid."

"Ghosts appear in many different ways, some with purpose, some without," Van said. "Knowing what it looks like, what you feel in the moment...all that helps to figure out their intentions and in turn how to communicate with them."

"Scared! I saw...Fuck! I saw my dead kid." Tears drooled out uncontrollably. This was why she hated talking about her feelings. Whenever she did, the anger, the frustration, the sadness, it poured out of her, leaked into the world and she couldn't stand it.

The desperation in Xander's bulging eyes came back to her. She recalled the need to be with him and the static of his absence. "I need to know if it's him. If it's *really* him."

*And I want to know if I can bring my son back and keep him here forever.* Some thoughts weren't meant to be shared.

Karina opened her front door to Clara and Van that evening. Van moved with the fluidity of a snake. They visually scanned the house, standing in the open-concept space that functioned as a foyer, kitchen, living room, and dining room. Van's expression was neutral, their palms out as if they could absorb the knowledge of what haunted Karina.

Clara sat at the island counter on a stool and popped open a can of mixed nuts that hadn't been opened for the funeral reception. "Just so you know, I think this is dangerous. You went through some bad shit and now you're *potentially* hallucinating. I think—" She looked to Van who closed their eyes and took a deep breath. "—you should see a therapist."

Karina opened her mouth to defend herself but Clara cut her off. "But, you're a friend, and I know this means a lot to you, so we'll try this one thing. We'll learn if what you're seeing is real, but no matter what happens, I want you to make an appointment, and I want you to do it before I leave tonight."

Karina nodded.

Van cast a blank expression in their direction, speaking in a low monotone. "I agree. Mental health is not something to take lightly. While communicating with our loved ones who've moved on can be incredibly therapeutic, it can also be hurtful."

"Okay, fine. I'll make an appointment. But for now...I mean...what do we do?"

"Do you ever feel Xander here?"

"I saw him in the bathroom."

"But do you *feel* him. You're a mother. Do moms know when their kid is in the room? Do you know that unmistakable presence? Or your husband? A smell? A touch."

"The night I saw him, I felt...I don't know."

"Describe it."

"Static. Or something."

Van's eyes narrowed. "Hmmm..." They walked slowly through the open space and nodded toward the hallway. "Do you mind?"

Karina gestured for them to explore.

Van floated ghostlike down the hallway toward the bedrooms and bathroom.

Clara rubbed her face in exhaustion. "How much time did they give you off of work?"

"They said I could take as much time as I need, but I'm losing my mind in this house. I don't know how much longer I can just stay here all day. I need to get back to work. I need to do *something*."

"Losing your mind is an understatement."

"You've never been one to pull punches, have you?"

"I pull back when I need to, but now's not that time."

"Now that I'm going crazy, you mean?"

Clara shrugged. "Do you really think Xander is here?"

A knife twisted in her heart. Believing her dead son was in her home made no sense, though she fiercely desired it to be true. "I don't know."

Clara chewed on her lip, perhaps pulling back those punches that would permanently knock Karina down. The punch delivering the reality that Karina's mind was broken, and none of what she'd seen was real.

Van reentered the kitchen and stood by the counter. "I'm sensitive to presences. I always have been. I can pick up on entities beyond our typical senses."

"And?" Clara asked.

"I don't think your son is here..." Van sucked their lips into a tight line. "But there's something..." They edged closer to Karina. "I don't know if it's close to you or kind of everywhere in the house."

"But not a ghost?"

"There are a lot of entities out there. Not just spirits of those who've passed, but things like demons."

"You think I have a demon?" Karina's trust in Van waned.

"No. I'm just saying that there's *something* here, but I can't figure it out. When did you start seeing the entity? Was it immediately after your husband and son passed? After the funeral?"

The image of the nebulous bear thing in the woods came to mind. How it stood upright watching her from between the trees on their drive up the mountainside a day before the accident. It was a dark secret that wasn't meant to be shared. Karina shrugged. "I don't remember."

"There's an energy here that I'm not familiar with. But spirits can manifest in a lot of different ways. They can be orbs of light, or shadows like you described. They can be cold spots, or a smell. They can be whatever we tell them to be, because they manifest from our own thoughts."

"What?" Clara roused from her boredom and cringed. "Manifest from our thoughts? That's called a hallucination."

"They're called thought-forms. But yeah, there's a lot of debate as to whether they're real or not."

The more Van spoke about things that didn't make sense, the farther the prospect of seeing Xander slipped away. If Van was suggesting the shadow figures and her vision of Xander were nothing more than her mind projecting his image, she didn't want to hear it. It was more than a hallucination: Karina *made* things happen, and she wouldn't give up on harnessing that power.

"What if I can project him back into reality?"

Clara slapped a hand on the counter. "Okay, I think we're done here. Xander is not a ghost in your house. He is a hallucination. And it's okay that you're not okay right now, but it's not okay for us to exacerbate the decline of your mental health by encouraging you to try to bring your deceased child back to life." Clara's voice crackled, and she choked on those last words. Her jaw tensed and her eyes became glassy, holding back tears.

"Nobody can come back from the dead, but there are many different possibilities when it comes to communicating with the spirits of loved ones. Not all spirits will be in their home. Some will go to school, or the hospital. Some will stay in the location where they died. Some manifest like an echo of a specific moment in time. Some manifest when they need to tell you something."

"Like what?" Karina asked.

"Like a secret or something they never told you."

Clara let out a sigh of frustration and stood, gathering her keys and bag.

Van intuited Clara's concern and their tone shifted. "Maybe it's not even Xander, but your need to know or to see something about him. Your need for the missing aspect, or maybe a need for closure is trying to bring him back. In that case, it could very well be only in your mind. You'd need to find peace if this manifestation of his image is ever going to rest."

"Yes, I agree with that last part," Clara said.

"But, it's weird. There's *something* here in the house, of that I'm certain. It's metallic, electric, like putting my tongue on the tip of a dead battery. I've never felt it before. I feel it when I'm near you." Van gazed into Karina as if they might see what's haunting her.

"So, Karina...since we've established whatever is haunting you is *not* Xander, or your husband, or any ghost for that matter, it's time to make that appointment with a psychologist."

In the morning, Karina canceled her online appointment. She wasn't ready to divulge the full extent of her insanity to anyone new. Not without exploring other options first. Instead, she did some online research about grief counseling and therapy, hoping to gain a few key phrases that she could spew at Clara if questioned about her sessions.

She read about the familiar "Five Stages of Grief" model of denial, anger, bargaining, depression, and acceptance. She also read that there's not much evidence to support it. She explored the "Four Tasks of Mourning" which includes accepting the reality, working through the pain, adjusting to life, and maintaining a connection to the deceased while moving on. *That last one.*

*Maintaining a connection while moving on.*

That's what she needed to do to heal, to move on, to do whatever society thinks is appropriate behavior after losing everything. She needed to maintain her connection with them, but it wasn't working here at home. No matter how many times she lay in Xander's bed, willing him back into her life, it wouldn't happen.

She stood in the bathroom mirror, and closed her eyes waiting for her son to return, standing behind her, but he never came. "Where are you?"

The doorbell rang.

If time could stop, Karina was certain it had. There was no sound, no light, no existence beyond her face in the mirror and whatever was waiting for her outside on the front porch. She couldn't recall how she managed to walk down the hallway to the front door, but now she stood with her hand on the cold knob, afraid to peek outside and scare away whatever she had conjured.

Karina held her breath and opened the door to her chatty neighbor, Shirley.

"Hey girl." Her eyes were wide and hungry, frantic to spill some neighborhood gossip.

It was stupid to believe she'd open the door to anything other than a living, breathing person.

Shirley looked down the street. "I'm just checking in to see how you're doing." She wore running leggings and a zippered athletic jacket. Her hair was tied back in a tight ponytail.

Karina shrugged. "It's early."

"I know, but..." She looked down the street.

Karina leaned out her door and followed her eyes to see several emergency vehicles blocking the street in front of Wendel's house.

"I thought you should know..."

Karina couldn't speak, she could only hold her breath and wait for whatever news Shirley had.

"Did you hear what happened?"

Karina shook her head.

Shirley let out a long sigh. "Wendel...you know Wendel..."

Her stomach flipped. "The guy who flirts with everyone."

"He committed suicide last night."

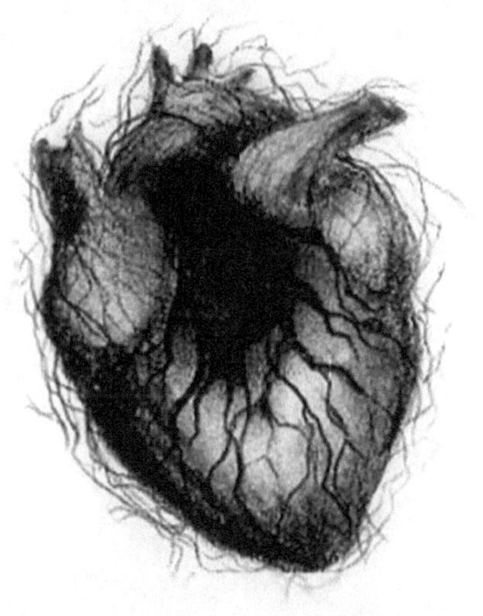

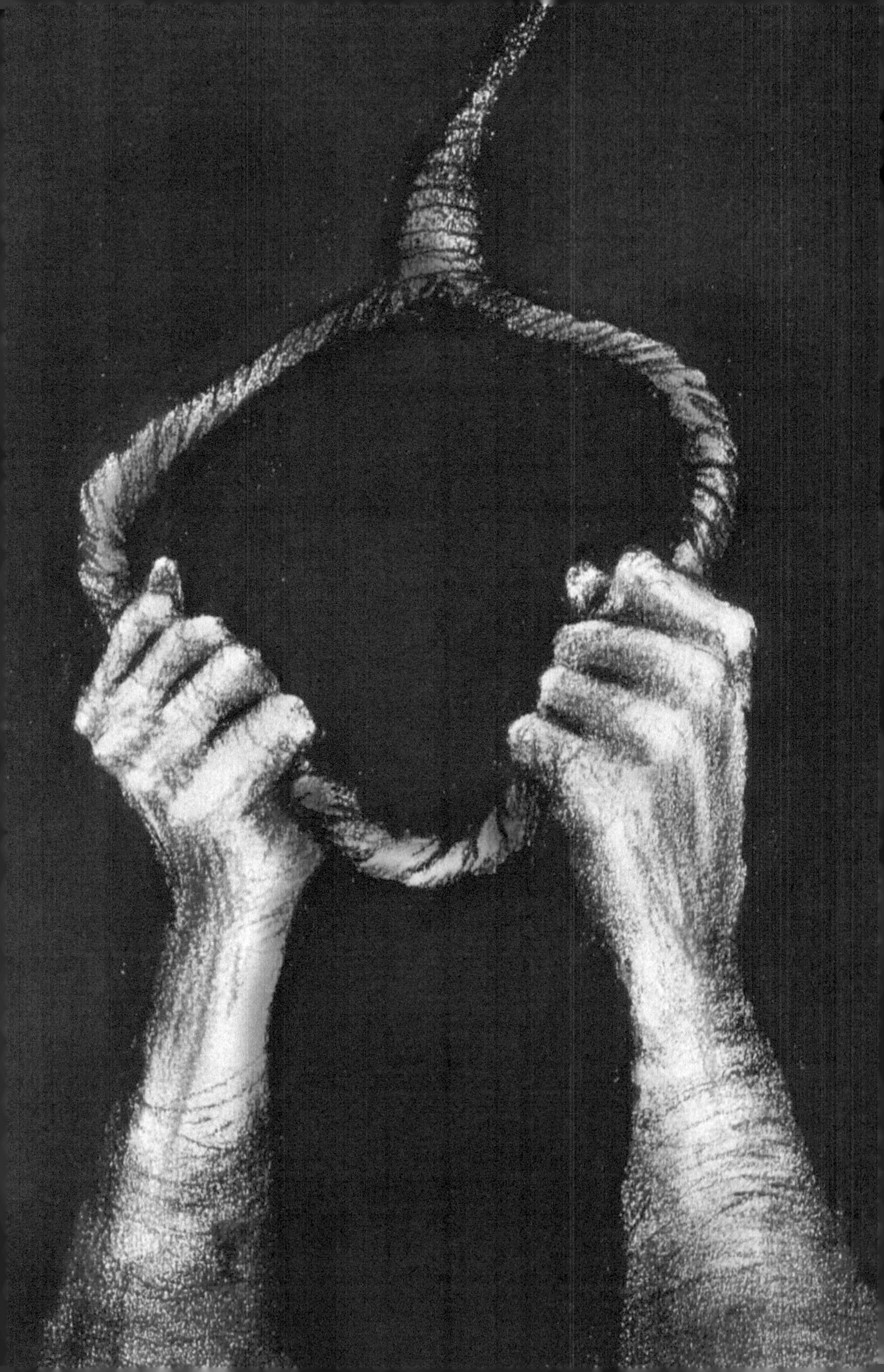

# CHAPTER 7

A cloud formed around Karina. A thick suffocating haze that made it impossible to breathe. She tried not to show the panic building.

Shirley's eyes were as wide as the gaping holes in Karina's soul. "The cops aren't saying anything official yet." She lowered her voice. "Dave, that hippie guy down at the end of the street, told me. He went to return the weed whacker he borrowed last week and when Wendel didn't answer the door, he went to the garage, and he found him." She whispered, placing a hand to her chest. "Hung himself."

Blood drained from her face and extremities faster than the blood that leaked from Xander's mouth. Her vision tunneled but she inhaled deeply through her nose, trying to maintain consciousness. A barely audible *oh my God* left her lips.

"I didn't even know he was...I didn't know he had those kinds of problems, you know?"

Karina moved onto the porch and stared down the street at Wendel's open garage door, at the gurney being wheeled out, body concealed in a bag.

"How have you been feeling, sweetheart?" Shirley tilted her head.

"I gotta go."

"Do you want some company? I can—"

"No."

Shirley couldn't hide her surprise over Karina's rejection.

Karina stepped inside her house. "It's just, I have a therapy appointment."

"Say no more." Shirley's hands went up. "I'll talk to you later, girl."

With her back against the door, she closed her eyes and tried to make sense of it all. She had one short daydream about Wendel hanging himself the other night. And it was barely a daydream at all. It didn't linger, it didn't return. It wasn't like the hundred times she'd imagined the home invasion as a child. Nor was it like the break-up of her parents, which she'd played in her head countless ways for months. Even though the death of her family did happen the day after a very specific dream, it wasn't the first time she'd imagined losing them forever.

But why Wendel? Why after one random passing daydream did it come true?

She ran back to the bathroom and tried to summon her kid into the mirror again, but he wasn't appearing.

*Come on, I can do this.*

*Exist.*

*Exist...*

Karina collapsed to the floor in tears. She curled like a fetus, lost and alone in the dark. The death toll of her imagination rose and she didn't know how to control it. There had to be a way. She buried the guilt of Wendel's death into the deepest recesses of her being so she could focus on harnessing her ability to make things happen. To *will* her son back into existence.

Van said there was something here in the house, but it wasn't Xander. That static spark was the shadow thing, and Karina knew it. But that didn't matter right now. All that mattered was finding and maintaining that connection to her boy, and it was clear she couldn't do it from her home, or he'd already be with her by now.

Xander had gone elsewhere.

Maybe she needed to go back to the mountains, to the crash site where she'd lost them. It was a long shot, but Van said some spirits remained where they died. And that mountain pass was the place where she'd first seen the shadow thing in the woods. They had to be connected. Thoughts spiraled uncontrollably. Reality and nonsense bled together, but all she could think to do was *go*.

The mountains were calling. *Xander* was calling. He beckoned her to investigate. Or maybe it was her own mind insisting she go to that crash site just in case there was some truth in Van's words. She'd go. She'd figure out how to see them again and how to fix the horrible thing she manifested.

She crudely packed a backpack and loaded the Subaru with essentials for an overnight trip to the Blue Ridge. From her house, it was about a four-and-a-half-hour drive.

The emergency vehicles down the street shrunk in her rearview mirror. The houses shrunk. The impossibility of the news about Wendel sat like a cinderblock in her chest.

Unsure what other options she had, Karina pulled onto the 264 highway ramp and headed west. She'd go to the mountains. If anything, it was best to get far away from the people in her life so she couldn't hurt anyone else.

All she could do was drive. Focus on the road, on not getting into a violent wreck. She shook the negative thoughts out of her head. Last thing she needed to do was spin off into a daydream about some horrible—

*No.*

*Think of the mountains. Think positive.* The morning fog clinging to the surface of rocks and dirt and trees. The feeling of breathing in the cloud of water vapor that would later dissipate, leaving bits of itself behind as dew. When she'd camped with her dad at The Peaks of Otter when she was a kid, they would wake early and climb Sharp Top Mountain so they could be above the low-lying clouds at the summit. The pair would be back to the bottom by noon when Mom was reading by the embers of the breakfast fire, enjoying her own version of peace.

Karina had wanted that for her family. It's strange. When you're a kid, you can filter out the bad memories and focus on the good. The memories of Dad retreating inward, losing his job, neglecting the house for weeks, months. Neglecting his family. Mom was right about Dad getting lost in the darkness, but Karina had trouble seeing that when she was young. She didn't see a lot of the problems regarding her childhood until she was old enough to look back with a more experienced eye.

*Mom* was the present and involved parent, but so much that she pushed Karina away from her interests. She loved writing, but every time Karina sat down at the computer to type out a story, Mom was there to edit her words. To careen her away from the stories she wanted to tell. In that way, Karina wasn't much different as a mother. Always trying to guide Xander in a way that she felt was best for him, rather than letting him explore what he wanted.

So much for positivity. There was no place for it in Karina's soul. She was doomed to live with regret, with guilt, with all things dark.

After a few hours of driving, the flat, shapeless coastal plains of southeastern Virginia gave way to hills, and then to the Blue Ridge Mountains. A light flickered inside of her when she saw the silhouette of those ancient rocks in the distance. The mountains felt like a home she could never claim. Even when she'd set up a tent and nestle within their embrace, it was temporary. A one-or-two-night stand before heading back to the home of her reality.

*What are you going to do now?* Mom had asked.

She didn't have to stay in Virginia Beach. The memory of her family soaked the walls like blood stains, and she could not endure it any longer. Would the stains fade and become a charm to the house that she loved? Or would they forever haunt her, reminding her of what she couldn't have?

She cracked a window and let the cool, wet spring air fill her lungs.

Maybe she could start a new home here, far away from everyone. Where her thoughts couldn't hurt a soul. Gavin's life insurance policy was enough to survive on for years if she sold the house and lived meagerly. She could buy a small cabin out in the middle of nowhere. Hike, and breathe, and finally have the life she'd always dreamed of. There'd be hardly any bills to pay; it's not like she had to worry about Xander's college tuition.

*What the fuck is wrong with you?*

How could she, a week after the funeral, think about how she'd spend her husband's life insurance money, and how convenient everything had become?

"I fucking hate you," she whispered.

Autopilot had kicked in and her body guided her to the mountains. But when I-64 cut across the Blue Ridge Mountain range, she snapped to attention from her wandering mind. The purple and blue peaks called for her to gaze upon them. They called for her to enter their forests and settle down for a rest. And she would be content to be lost within them.

According to the GPS, the fastest way to the crash site was to cut over the mountains on I-64, travel south to Buchanan, then cut east back over the mountains on the windy road where they'd lost control of the vehicle. It was the same route Gavin had driven two weeks earlier. She stopped in Buchanan to fill her tank and to take a moment to think about whether or not she had the strength to continue.

She didn't let the thought linger for long. Her Subaru lurched up the steep mountain incline. The fracture in her arm ached as she attempted using only fingers to guide the steering wheel, but extending her arm, even for brief periods, caused too much stress on the bone. She needed to steer with one arm as much as possible. The ascent was slow, careful. Each switchback dangled their dead faces before her. The memory of Gavin at the wheel and her annoyance with the squealing of the brake pads rang like a ghost in her ear. The arguing. She looked over her shoulder, picturing Xander in the backseat, face in his sketchbook. Hood up.

Karina knew exactly which switchback to go to. After the accident, she'd pulled up a map of the area and played the events in her head over and over. She envisioned herself as a bird rather than the satellite that took the imagery on the map. She neared the corner, slowed, and noted a new guard rail already in place. On the narrow roads with no shoulder, she couldn't simply park anywhere. Instead, she waited for the next dirt pull-off area about fifty yards up the mountain from the turn and parked safely off the road.

Traffic was sparse on the mountain pass. She'd only seen one other vehicle. The town of Buchanan sat at one end of the road, and at the top of the mountain was the Blue Ridge Parkway. Beyond the Blue Ridge Parkway was the Peaks of Otter Lodge, and down the road, a primitive campground.

She exited her car and walked the shoulder-less road down to the sharp corner.

It replayed in her head as flashes. Gavin's white knuckles. His foot mashing into the brake pedal. She reached the guard rail and looked down into the steep ravine. The slope was gradual enough that she could navigate on foot if she was careful to hold onto the trees. The car was no longer there. It'd been hooked and fished out the day of the crash. About a hundred yards down the slope, beyond a plowed path of weeds, brush, and broken twiggy growth, a massive pine tree stood. The tree that killed her family.

That's where she needed to be. She had to be where they died. She had to hold her palms up, like Van had done in her home, and try to *feel* them. This time, instead of static, instead of that metallic dead battery, perhaps she'd sense them. Maybe she'd sit with their ghosts and dream up a way to bring them back. Karina held to branches with her one good arm, and made her descent. Her hiking boots scraped away topsoil and moss, kicking up a mist of petrichor on her way down.

There was damage to the bark of the pine tree where their vehicle had been stopped. She placed her hand on the tree's scar and waited to feel them, to see them, but nothing happened.

Karina leaned against the tree. She zipped her hoodie and sat, unsure what else to do other than return to her dream of a life with them. She could build a cabin right here. Gavin and Xander might not be alive, but they could be with her in spirit. As orbs of light or something. She'd hike with Xander through the forest, and though she wouldn't be able to hug him, to hold him, she'd feel that he was happy. She wouldn't stare into lifeless eyes, but instead eyes of light. Aglow, flitting through the forest the way she did as a child, content. And then she'd lay in bed at night in the dark of the forest and while Xander slept peacefully, her husband would fill her with luminous kisses. His lack of form would not leave her body feeling neglected though. His light would touch her in places, fulfilling every void with pleasure.

There would be no more darkness, only light. The light of her family who were taken away. It was a morbid little dream, but thinking about it made her the happy.

*Make it happen.*

*How?*

Did she just need to wait for tomorrow? She stood, brushing away earth from her bottom, and noticed a black rectangular void near her foot. It peeked out from under some freshly sprouted ferns. She lifted it from the mud. A black sketchbook.

Karina held it to her chest and for a moment it felt like it was him. Like her infant boy, warm and helpless, had nuzzled against her breast and fallen asleep. She cradled him against her, feeling each beat of her pulse against the hard cover of the sketchbook, like chest compressions pumping life back into her baby.

"Come back to me," she whispered.

She didn't realize how much she loved him until he was gone. What kind of mother did that make her? What kind of mother doesn't immediately love their child? Karina never spoke about it because it felt wrong. Because nobody says those things. Because love is supposed to be instinctual, but for Karina, it didn't come until later. The need to protect was there. The need to take care of him was inescapable. But the love, the bond, was not immediate. It was hard.

She opened the sketchbook, a previously forbidden act. Some pages were glued together with mud and rain, but she flipped through the water-damaged pages that she could peel apart. He was a creative soul with line art sketches of demons and dragons and monsters devouring flesh. Detailed drawings of all things macabre. His talent was applauded in school, though some of his art was too graphic for contests and art shows. But Xander had a small following online, and for good reason. He was talented, maybe even better than her father. Dad was so good he'd landed some big-name publications months before the first stroke.

She flipped a page to see a drawing of her dad, decrepit, slack-jawed, wearing the god-awful tracksuit with a few scattered blue and orange marks to denote its color. Dad's face had a line of drool drawn from his lip to the floor. His wife stood behind him with marionette strings attached. A thought bubble over Dad read, "I'm trapped."

It caught Karina off-guard. She had no idea Xander felt this way, or even noticed the way Mom took control of Dad's life after the stroke. Dad had no way of making decisions for himself, and Xander saw that.

She flipped another page to see word art accompanying images of his gym teacher, an over-muscled monster in school colors screaming.

The next page stole her breath. It reached into her throat with claws and squeezed until she gave up on trying to fight for air. It was a drawing of Karina, scribbled as black, jagged lines. An inky center, black scratched-out eyes, angry brows turned down at the bridge of the nose. She held college applications in her hand, one finger pointing to a clock with a thought balloon saying, "Hurry up and get out of my life." As wallpaper behind the drawing, the words FUCK YOU MOM FUCK YOU MOM FUCK YOU MOM…were written like a delinquent child's lines on a chalkboard. At least five across and dozens of rows down. *FUCK YOU, MOM.*

Her son's final thoughts were painted into the folds of her memory forever. She read every line, absorbed each hate-filled scratch of the pen and sank into the earth, ready to die alongside them.

All else went numb except for the searing pain of Xander's words lacerating the scar tissue trying to form inside her. Why would he ever want to come back to her?

The scramble up the loamy soiled slope was a haze. Her broken arm screamed as she grabbed young saplings for support. For brief seconds, it eclipsed the pain within. She sat in her car on the side of the road clutching Xander's sketchbook, begging for forgiveness. Dreaming every possible scenario where she could have him back and make things right, but she'd need to stay the night and give it time to come true.

Karina put the car in gear and left the site of the accident behind her. It was late afternoon by the time she reached the campground. There was nobody at the ranger station, so she followed the camping honor system and left the twenty-dollar fee in an envelope before picking her site.

A few other primitive campers had set up, scattered across the grounds, lone hikers or travelers dropping in for one night. On a cool Wednesday afternoon in the spring, she could expect there wouldn't be many more people trickling in.

It was a struggle putting up the dome tent with only one fully-functional arm, but she managed to use her right hand to help with some of the tasks, even though using that side for anything brought waves of pain shooting up through her elbow all the way to her shoulder.

Karina mindlessly set up camp and sat by a cold empty fire pit with no flames, staring into the ash with a lifeless gaze.

*What are you going to do now?*

She'd think of nothing but Xander, and force him back into existence. Her stomach grumbled, and she realized she hadn't consumed anything but a cup of coffee that morning. She hadn't been eating much of anything since the accident. It was getting late, the sun would be setting soon, and the camp store down the road at the base of Sharp Top was closed. She could head down to the lodge and sit at the restaurant alone, but the thought of eating turned her stomach. Hunger bit at her insides, stomach acid gurgled, but she denied it a meal.

*You don't deserve to eat.*

She brought the empty coffee cup down the hill near the restroom where there was a pump for fresh water. The last time she walked this path was with Gavin after making love in the tent.

Now, she walked to the bathroom alone. The woods were already darkening as the dying daylight became trapped in the branches of mountainside trees. The darkness stole away the bright greens of the freshly budded forest and replaced it with a dull gray hue. She checked over her shoulder to be sure nobody had followed the lone woman into the bathroom, but saw only tall trees, gnarled brush, and shadow.

Inside, the lights flicked on, and Karina went to the same stall, the larger, wheelchair-accessible one with the creepy ventilation windows at the base of the wall. She recalled imagining a face poking through last time she sat on that seat. Those ventilation holes stared at her, taunted her, threatened to show her things she had no interest in seeing. But it was either use the toilet or go squat in the woods.

So, she sat down and relaxed enough to let her bladder go. As the trickle of urine began, a rustle on the ground outside came from the ventilation hole. It forced her to clench off the flow. She paused, listening to the sound of dirt and shuffling—a slithering noise moved outside. Something much larger than a snake.

Karina relaxed her bladder and forced out the stream as fast as possible. As she finished, the noise grew louder and a dark shadow thing blocked the hole near her feet. It was coming in.

However, instead of the ambiguous black smudge, a bulbous hairy thing squeezed through. Short brown hairs parted to reveal wounds, fresh and pink, exposing flesh and the necrotic edges of aging injuries. A long fissure ran along a pale forehead, which led to an eyebrow. A familiar brow, dark and thick. As the man's head squeezed unnaturally through the window at her feet, Gavin's eyes met hers. He squeezed his head in farther, nose and mouth coming into view. Bits of brain matter bulged from a broken skull and crumbled, tumbling down his face.

Her reaction was swift, but clumsy. She rocketed off the toilet, using her one good arm to pull her pants up on one side. A scream crawled up her throat and she didn't know what else to do but defend herself from the monstrosity fighting to squeeze through a too-small hole. Though it had Gavin's face, there was absolutely nothing *Gavin* about his dead, prying eyes. She kicked at it but it kept staring. She stomped, and stomped again, and again.

As she screamed, her voice seemed to disappear, universe collapsing to a pinhole and all that existed was her foot, sinking sinking sinking into the fissure in his forehead. Scraps of brain and blood and meat clung to her hiking boot and to her ankle as she pulled her foot from his crushed skull.

Karina ran, without all of her ass inside her pants. The bathroom door flung open and she collided with a flannel wall of a human. She screeched again, certain it was Gavin, or the thing pretending to be Gavin. Sparks shot up her broken arm toward her elbow on impact, and those sparks appeared as stars behind her tightly squeezed eyes when she flinched.

He threw up his hands in surrender and backed away. Karina yanked her pants up, and the man's face came into focus. He was a tall, dark-haired man, clean-shaven with a small tactical style hatchet, held to the side unthreateningly. As he met her panicked eyes, he set it down on the ground.

"Whoa! What's happening?" he said.

She backed away from the bathroom with her hands over her mouth.

"Is there something in there?" He picked up the hatchet and grabbed the handle of the ladies' room. Before pulling it open, he stalled. "There's not like a bear in here, is there?"

Karina's teeth chattered; the imagery couldn't be shaken. The sensation of Gavin's, or the Gavin thing's brain on her boot and ankle remained. When she looked at her feet, though, there was no sign of trauma. No blood, no chunks of flesh. She regained some level of outward composure and shook her head. "It was nothing."

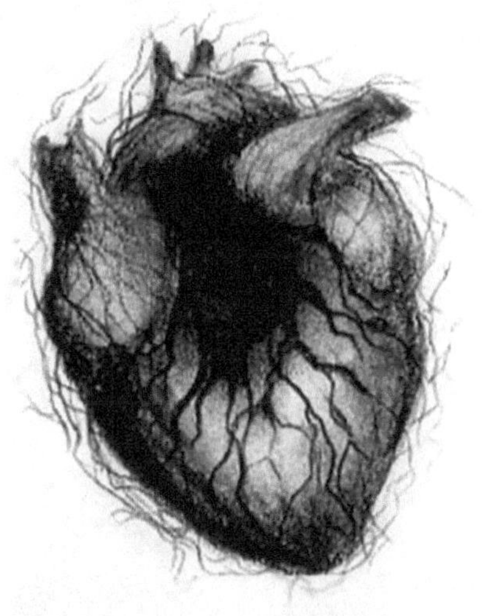

# CHAPTER 8

The hatchet-wielding man gave a knock on the ladies' room door and poked his head inside. He disappeared for only a few seconds, then came back outside laughing. "You scared the shit outta me, lady. What the hell was that all about? You see a snake or something?"

Karina nodded. "Yeah. I think so."

"Shit, I thought you were being murdered, the way you screamed. You good?"

Karina could only nod as her face drained of blood. She took a deep breath and tried to derail any concerns. "I'm fine. Just an irrational fear. Snake-o-phobia... or whatever."

The man laughed. "Ophidiophobia. My mom has it. She grew up in Brazil. She lived in a city, but still, when she was a little girl, a massive snake managed to get into her house. She woke up with it in her bed. She's been scared of them ever since."

His voice was a distant thing, a muffled noise that didn't matter. Karina gradually stepped back toward the corner of the bathhouse to get a look on the other side. Metal grates, not much more than chicken wire, covered each ventilation hole with the exception of the hole closest to the toilet. That one remained wide open. The soil outside appeared freshly disturbed.

Did she just stomp her husband out of existence the second she got him back? She swallowed the bile trying to eject itself from her insides.

"Bet it slithered out through that hole. You want me to walk you back to your campsite?"

Karina sealed herself shut. "No! I'm fine."

Karina wasn't sure she could handle being alone all night in her tent. She drove down the road and sat in the lodge parking lot as the sun set, considering whether or not to get a room. Her phone erupted with messages dinging through rapid-fire now that she had a signal. A few from her mom, asking how she was doing. No apologies though. The other texts were from Clara.

*Van has been obsessed with you.*

*They've been researching ghosts and demons and shit.*

*They've been talking to their mother about you...weird...I know.*

*Where are you?*

*Anyway, they said you should look into doing some shadow work. It's some Carl Jung philosophical thing about facing our dark sides.*

*Seriously, text me back or I'm going to have to come over there tomorrow and check on you.*

What would Karina say if she called or texted back? That she's in the mountains alone trying to connect with her dead family and she's so fucking close? That now, so many terrible things she imagines are actually happening? She pressed her palms against her eyes until the blackness sparked with the red and white spots. Like the cosmos came alive in her head. Deep breaths filled her lungs and pressed against her fractured heart. What if she stayed here in the darkness, with her imagined stars...

*Don't imagine anything, you idiot.*

Karina opened her phone and searched Carl Jung as Van suggested. She skimmed a few online articles, learning about a darkness within all of us, a shadow-self. But the philosophical idea was a metaphor. Not a physical entity.

She clicked on Clara's name and punched the green phone button to dial. It rang only once and Clara answered. "Hey girl..."

Karina didn't know where to begin, so she pulled the phone away from her ear and considered hanging up.

Clara didn't wait for a reply. "I texted you a few times."

"I just got them. Thanks."

"Where've you been? Your mom said you weren't home today."

"I'm allowed to leave the house...I'm grieving, not a prisoner."

"Yeah, but you have people who are worried about you. Why couldn't you respond?"

"I didn't have a signal."

"Where are you that you don't have a signal?" Clara's tone was sharp, maternal.

"Look, I got your texts about the shadow thing. What's happening to me is too...real."

"I was just relaying Van's thoughts. They were pretty convincing. You've been through some shit, Karina. And you lock it all up inside. It's not good for you."

"Clara, I lied to you."

Clara didn't reply.

Karina put the phone on speaker and set it down on the console. She gripped the steering wheel with her good hand and placed the other in her lap. The façade of the lodge was lit in the foreground of Sharp Top Mountain, looming in the distance like an enormous shadow itself, silhouetted against the darkening sky. If Karina said anymore, she'd sound batshit crazy, but she needed to tell someone or she might combust. A sigh escaped her lips. "I lied when I told you I didn't foresee the accident. The day before it happened, I had a very detailed daydream."

Clara still said nothing. Her silence a weight. A thick curtain between them.

Karina closed her eyes, biting her lip, awaiting Clara to say something—anything.

"When you say 'detailed' what do you mean?" she asked.

"I mean exactly how they died, right down to the injuries."

"Are you fucking with me?"

Karina knew she didn't need to reply to that. She waited for her to say anything else.

"I'm coming over."

"No. You can't."

"Why not?"

"I'm not home..."

"Where are you?"

"I drove to the Blue Ridge to see the crash site."

"Jesus Christ. Alone?"

"I'm so close to seeing them." Her voice broke, cracking open like a busted valve.

"What do you mean?"

Karina regained control. "I thought I'd feel them. I thought maybe, well, I don't know what I thought. But I keep seeing Xander and Gavin. Horrible visions, but they're here. Somehow the shadow thing makes it happen. I think."

"That's not possible."

"No shit! If I thought it was possible, I wouldn't be so freaked out right now! And whether I believe it's possible or not doesn't matter, because it's happening. All the things I imagine, everything but bringing them back. I don't know what to do."

Clara's tone softened. "Okay, I'm going to get Van and we're going to work through this together. You're going to be fine. We'll get you a counselor, or a medium or a psychic, a fucking shaman or a priest or whatever the fuck you need, okay?"

Karina didn't know why she bothered to call anyone. No help could come from another person. The help she required came from the shadow. Whether anyone believed it was real or not, she'd harness that dead-battery energy Van tasted on their lips and make it work to her advantage.

She couldn't remember the rest of the conversation, Karina's head was elsewhere. Clara offered Van's theories, something about her false sense of guilt haunting her. The taste of culpability on her tongue made her stomach gurgle. She'd be lying to everyone, including herself if she didn't admit that sometimes she wished she never had a family. Countless occasions after Xander had been born, even before he was born, she'd wished to live alone in the mountains with no obligations other than caring for her own well-being. A crazy old hermit in the wilderness, a haggard old forest witch. Her memory of Gavin's voice in the pitch black, disturbed by her twisted imagination, brought a smile to her face. Gavin often claimed she was selfish, and though she argued she'd given everything of herself to their family, there was some truth to his words. If ever there was a time to be selfish, it was now. She was so close to making everything right again, and she wasn't going to let Clara's paranoia keep her from doing it.

At some point, she hung up and drove back toward the campground.

She pulled into the campground and the flannel man from earlier was leaning against the ranger station, one arm up, appearing to flirt with the ranger, a petite woman with long dark hair.

"Hey! That's her!" the flannel man said.

"Good evening!" the ranger said, waving for her to stop. She approached Karina's vehicle.

Karina came to a stop before the speed bump.

"See anymore snakes?" the man asked.

The woman smiled. "Hi! Did you get settled in alright?"

"Yes..."

Her name tag read: *Isabelle Delgado*. She was young, couldn't be out of her twenties "Jason was just telling me about a snake that got into the bathhouse."

Karina nodded, blinking away the image of her husband's crushed face from her mind. "It was nothing, really."

"Do you know what kind of snake it was? What color? Just wanna make sure it wasn't one of the dangerous ones."

Karina avoided the question about the snake she'd never seen. "It wasn't anything to worry about. I'm fine. Everything's fine." She held her foot pressed to the brake pedal, eager to get moving again.

He approached the car with an extended hand. He was handsome, possibly a decade younger than her, and he reminded her of a lumberjack, the LL Bean kind, but surprisingly a little rugged from the trail. His shirt constricted around biceps as he shook her hand.

"I'm Jason."

"Karina," she said.

"So, the snake…" Isabelle held out her hands about two feet apart, extending slowly to suggest size.

"It was no big deal…" Karina faked a smile. "…a little thing. Black, I think."

"Okay," Isabelle said. "I'll put in a work order to have the grate returned to the ventilation gap, but, Nature, you know? I'm staying this week in the camper up the hill." She pointed behind her, toward loop A. "It's the only camper up there. So if you have any bigger snakes and need help, feel free to come knocking."

Jason scratched the nape of his neck. "I'm down there at the curve in loop B. So, same. Feel free if you have any trouble."

"Believe it or not, I'm not a stranger to camping," Karina said.

After a spell of silence, Isabelle broke it with an awkward, "Okay! I'm heading to my camper. Good night."

Jason made a subtle bow to Karina as she removed her foot from the brake and pulled away. She couldn't gauge the steely glare of Jason's eyes. Was he flirting? It'd been so long since someone had come on to her, she forgot how to tell. His eyes landed upon Isabelle the same way, so perhaps it was simply a certain swagger he had. Or, he was a lone hiker on the Appalachian Trail who was looking for a one-night stand from either of them.

Headlights shone down loop B, guiding her to her campsite. Her flashlight navigated the short gravel path to her tent. Soon after, Jason walked by on the paved path, heading on foot toward his site farther down loop B.

"Hello again!" he waved, but the charcoal gray evening was so dark, his form was difficult to distinguish from the backdrop of the forest. She waved back as he continued down the paved path, disappearing in the encroaching night. For a moment, he appeared to be a shadow. A foggy patch of darkness that she'd grown accustomed to seeing far too frequently lately.

The time had come to grab the reins of her thoughts and keep them under control. Her most innocuous, wandering bad thoughts became reality. Not the things she truly wanted. Tricking her mind into bringing Xander or Gavin back was the only reasonable option she had.

She lay alone in her tent, at first avoiding the dive into the darkest recesses of her mind. She couldn't bear to hurt anyone else, to lose anyone else. What if she'd let her mind slip away and something happened to Clara or her mother? It was too difficult to live with herself, and hurting another person would push her over the edge. But each time she imagined Gavin or Xander, it wasn't how they should've been remembered. It was the graphic imagery of their deaths. It was blood and gore which brought no peace. And that's all she wanted, if only for a moment. Peace. If she could close her eyes and fall asleep right now she would. Karina would slip into a dream, of mountain fog and her haggard self in the woods alone. And never wake up. This would be her afterlife. Maybe there, she'd see Gavin and Xander as something other than mangled flesh.

She heard footsteps on the pavement outside her tent. They shuffled by without slowing, without coming up the gravel path toward her. Likely just a camper heading toward the bathhouse. Or maybe it was Jason, patrolling the loop, looking to rescue some damsel from rogue snakes. She pictured him coming to her tent. His chiseled face wouldn't smile. Instead, he'd gaze longingly, knowing all she really wanted from a man in this moment was an orgasm. She wondered if the rest of his body was cut like a statue of a Greek god as well.

Karina was lonely. Her nerves sparked to attention, craving touch. It was the best part of her relationship with Gavin, how he made her come, the upside of so many years together. Guilt nipped at her for even considering being with someone else, but Jason was the perfect stranger to imagine hovering over her body. Shirtless, nipples hard from the chill in the air. His hands, his lips, his skin would explore her body and she'd let him. Why not? It's not like she's married anymore. She pushed the heartless sentiment out, taking a moment to honor the memory of her husband, but he never looked like *that*. Jason pulsed over her, hips swiveling, fitting her with what was hopefully a well-sized package. Afterward, she watched him chop wood, shirtless by a raging fire. The blade would blast through a log and split it in two, the way he'd split her legs with his powerful thrust. The throbbing between her legs ached for it to be reality. Then, she'd send him away, because that would be all she needed from him. And as she slept, Jason might return, yearning in his eyes for something different. An axe raised over her slumbering body, because, he was a psychopath who had lowered her guard so he could return and...

Before her mind dragged her to those fucked up places, she came to her senses. There'd be no daydreaming about axes tonight.

Just in case, Karina locked herself in her vehicle. She moved her thoughts to *her* men, focused on their faces and dreamed of a world where they could be with her. The Subaru wasn't very comfortable, but she slept most of the night, only waking a few times to what felt like an abyss trapped outside of time. So much darkness she curled into a ball and closed her eyes so tight that she could see stars again.

It was the shadow surrounding her. Filling the car and the campground.

*Bring them back to me.*

Scant predawn light permeated the vehicle, and she woke in a blanket of fog so thick she couldn't spot her tent, which was only about ten yards away up the hill. The ghosts of her family were rotting and sticky inside her. They were like crude oil lining her lungs, suffocating, and her body wanted them out. But that shadow wouldn't let them leave.

*What am I doing wrong?*

She opened her car door and the wet, mountain air filled her lungs. There was no room inside for the joy of a lungful of mountain air. Instead, she stepped away from the car and onto the paved path of loop B. She hated to go back down to the bathhouse to use the toilet after what she'd seen the night before, but she needed to relieve herself. Down the drive, a silhouette came into view. After the intense daydream she had of Jason last night, she wouldn't mind that one coming true.

The silhouette of his figure grew as he approached, carrying the hatchet in his right hand, hanging to his side.

She stood in the middle of the paved road and waved. Her voice sleepily cracked. "Good morning."

Jason didn't reply. As his silhouette drew closer, she could make out the details of his outfit. Jeans and a Carhart jacket. Blue flannel collar underneath. A stony face, calm and emotionless, stared through her, but not at her. His eyes were unfocused, dark. It wasn't the haze of the fog that kept her from seeing his irises. They were clouded, near-black, like storm clouds. There was no feeling, no expression, a zombie.

She took a step back.

Jason stopped his approach and his chest rose and fell subtly with each breath. A breath as calm and deep as someone who was asleep.

Jason raised his axe over his head, dead eyes hooked into Karina as his target.

He moved his other hand to double grip the axe and lunged, but Karina had already taken off in a sprint down loop B toward the ranger station.

She screamed, wondering if anyone would see the attempted assault or if it was in her head. Clara could be right. It could all be imagined and all she needed to do was stop running and face it head on. Prove to herself that it was only a hallucination. But the hatchet, the look in his eyes, the smell of sweat on his skin and mud on his hiking boots was all too real. She couldn't risk it.

"Help!" Her toes pressed into pavement and pushed off, sprinting as fast as she could, nearly failing to hold back her need to pee. Behind, Jason held his hatchet in both hands, running, ready to slash into her.

Nobody crawled from their tents to see the commotion. Bystander effect lessons rushed back so she yelled, "Fire!"

She gained distance.

"Bear!" Anything to get the few scattered campers out of their tents. She reached the shuttered ranger station, then cut up the hill.

Her screams gained volume, but the louder she screamed, the slower her pace became, closing the gap between her and Jason.

Grainy images, streaked with red, from dozens of Dad's favorite 80s slasher movies, played on a loop. The tripping, stumbling campers, and she would surely be one as she scaled the hillside wood plank-steps which cut up a steep slope to loop A.

She reached Isabelle's camper and pounded on the locked door. "Hey!"

Jason closed in, so she stepped down from the camper steps and backed away, deciding if it was smarter to run into the woods or remain on the paved loops.

A stocky, short man with a beard trailed Jason. Crouched like a hunting lion, he sped his pace for the last few yards and tackled him from behind, arms wrapped around Jason's torso and arms. They both went down, and Jason's face smacked into the pavement. The stocky man wrestled the hatchet out of his grip.

Isabelle finally opened the door, her jacket over her pajamas.

Jason was on all fours, wavering.

The stocky man threw the hatchet to the side and pulled a pistol from under his pant-leg. "Stay there, asshole!"

Jason put his hands up. His eyes were clear and brown again, like they'd been the day before. His face was full of fear, confusion, full of *life*, like he'd suddenly woken from nightmare.

# CHAPTER 9

She didn't wait for the cops to come. She didn't bother packing up her tent. As Jason stammered on about sleep-walking, Karina dashed back to her Subaru with no destination in mind. Her condition was spiraling into something that she couldn't control. She needed to get away from people as soon as possible before she began thinking about other horrible things regarding the ranger, Isabelle, or the mysterious stocky man, or...

She peeled out of the campground, Isabelle trying to wave her down, refusing to engage. Her chest felt so tight it was difficult to breathe, panic setting in. Hyperventilating. Her vision narrowed to a small tunnel. Instead of continuing, she took a sharp left turn into the camp store parking lot at the base of Sharp Top trail.

Her phone dinged with incoming messages. Each chime accompanied an onslaught of realizations.

*Ding.* You made that man attack you. *Ding.* You took away his free will. *Ding.* You're a fucking monster. *Ding.* You are selfish. *Ding Ding Ding Ding Ding Ding*

Just kill yourself and rid the world of your evil.

She parked facing a narrow, grassy field butting up against the far edge of the campground. She'd run across it as a little girl, climbed the steps by the trailhead center, and hiked the grueling trail with her dad. They reached the top after two hours, where massive diorite boulders sat above the trees, steps crudely carved allowing passage to the highest point overlooking mountains and valleys for miles. She'd leaned against the carved wall with her dad to take in the view. That was before his depression took over. Before he leapt into a pit of darkness beyond the reach of helping hands.

Dad withdrew from the light, withdrew from his family. Now that Karina's family was gone, she understood her father even less. How could he do that? How could he choose to live without her and Mom? No matter how much she dreamed about being without her family, she never wanted it to actually happen. The pity and despair in her gut became resentment and anger. Hatred for her father's refusal to stay present. To be a father, a husband, a grandpa.

Maybe her mother had been right all along; Karina wasn't great at relationships. It was in her DNA. A genetic aversion to love. She couldn't even love her baby as a mother should. And no matter how hard she tried to play the normal, functioning person with a family, she'd become just like her father, longing for solitude. Longing for it so much she made it happen. Then she killed Wendel. And if she continued on this path, she would kill off everyone in an attempt to bring back a family already lost to her. The shadow thing was in control.

If the shadow was bound to her, Karina was a danger to everyone, and it was time to do something *unselfish* and rid the world of her darkness.

*Riiiing...*

Karina was wilted, sallow and weak, but it was her mother calling and she deserved whatever she had to say. One more conversation. One more chastising rant about how horrible of a person Mom believed Karina to be. "Hi Mom."

"Oh, Thank God you answered. Where have you been?"

"Does it matter?"

Mom paused for a few seconds.

"I need to show you something."

"Now's not a good time."

"It's about your dad. I found something of his. A journal. It's..."

Karina waited for her mom to go on, but the sentence trailed into an abyss of silence.

"A journal?"

"Will you please swing by and see this? It's urgent."

"I can't."

"Why not?"

"I'm about to hike this mountain—"

"Mountain?! What are you doing out there?"

"I'm taking your advice."

"What are you talking about?"

"You said I need to do something before someone else got hurt, right?"

"Karina..."

"I have to go now."

"Your father had it too!" Mom interjected.

After a delay, purposeful or not, Karina asked, "Had what?"

"In this journal, every other week or so, there's an entry about how he worried he'd have a stroke or a heart attack and leave without..." she trailed off again into a place her words couldn't manage to form. "He wrote about his stroke before it happened. I didn't even know he worried about that. He was healthy."

"What are you saying?"

"I'm saying whatever this is that you have, this ability to make things happen. Your father had it too and—"

Karina hung up without knowing why. Maybe she couldn't bear to hear her mother's voice. Or she couldn't handle what she'd heard. Or she was too damned tired to deal with any of it. She muted her phone and threw it in the back seat.

Where the grassy field severed the forest into a straight line, towering trees stretched long shadows in the fog. Among those shadows was hers. The inky nebula, writhing and hungry to plagiarize her imagination for its own entertainment. A pair of middle-aged women walked along the sidewalk, heading toward the steps that led to the Sharp Top trail. They paused for a moment and stared into the tree line where the shadow thing lurked. One of the women, wearing hiking boots and shorts, pointed. Karina couldn't hear what she said, but the other adjusted her line of sight.

Karina stepped out of the vehicle.

The woman in shorts asked, "Did you see that?"

The shadow thing slipped into the forest. Karina watched the black patch move up the steep hillside and out of sight.

The taller woman wearing shorts and a backpack said, "I hope it wasn't a bear. That's the last thing we need is to run into a bear on the trail."

Her hiking partner wore pink leggings and a ball cap through which her blonde ponytail swished back and forth as she ascended.

Gnarled roots snaked across the trail, catching Karina's foot and occasionally making her trip. She'd lost sight of the shadow, but couldn't leave it to wander the mountain. It would do something terrible. What if it were to slither through the trees and push those two women up ahead from one of the ledges on their climb? Or perhaps it might seep into the mountain soil, wriggle through the packed dirt around granite and diorite and into the roots of the trees along the trail. It could do whatever it wanted. It could make anything happen. It could control the roots of the trees and catch on the women's ankles, yanking them into the ground so deep that their...

*Fuck.* She bashed the heel of her palm into her temple. *Stop it!*

She had to catch up to them before the shadow did. Karina sprinted at first, but her legs twitched, threatening to cramp on the steep incline. Her sprint turned to a jog, and then a shuffle. Her thighs screamed. The pain became a source of motivation, a suggestion of what might happen to others if she failed. The soft, loamy earth became hard, packed dirt; exposed rock and massive root systems created an unsteady path up the mountain.

Screams echoed off boulders, surrounding her, and she ran toward the source. The two shrieking voices were reminiscent of Karina's outburst upon seeing Gavin's mangled skull wriggle through the bathroom ventilation hole. The sound of terror, of someone who'd seen or experienced something that made them question reality.

Karina rounded the bend in the path and found them. The ball cap woman's torso was all that was visible at the outside edge of the trail near a boulder the size of a pickup truck. She had sunk into the soil, roots twisted around her arms and neck.

The woman in shorts was soaked in tears, arms and legs wrapped around her friend to keep her from going under.

"Stop!" Karina screamed. "Leave them alone!" She dove to the ground and tore at the roots, ripping them away as more roots squirmed from the soil and lunged for the woman's head.

"It's okay, Melissa...we got you." She looked to Karina. "Go get help!"

"There is no help. I didn't imagine the end of this daydream." Karina spoke to the shadow, "I haven't written it yet."

Karina closed her eyes and finished the story in her mind.

The roots relaxed and the ponytailed woman's squirming made the soil shift.

"Thank God," the friend said, digging away at the topsoil with her fingers.

"Jay...I still feel it on my ankles. It's pulling."

Precisely as Karina had planned, the soil at the edge of the slope opened, roots yanking her down into the earth, ripping her away from her friend and dragging her through worms and decaying forest leaves.

Jay's arms reached into the massive rabbit hole left behind where her friend had disappeared. "Melissa!"

Karina climbed the pickup sized boulder and neared the edge, looking downhill. "Wait for it..."

An explosion of dirt spewed from the side of the hill below, and the pink blur that was Melissa was cannoned out. She crashed against a massive pine and her body collapsed to the ground, bloody and broken.

Jay screamed. Her hands trembled near her face.

"It's okay!" Karina smiled, lips dry and cracked. Blood bloomed and she licked it away. The roots had done as she'd imagined. "She's alive."

"She's alive, asshole!" Karina shouted into the forest, hoping the shadow would hear her.

Jay stood staring at Karina, mouth agape.

Laughter bubbled up from her gut and into the woods. "This is my story!" *And I know exactly how it ends.*

"Can I tell you how it ends?" she asked the stranger, Jay, who scrambled down the hillside to be with her partner.

Karina followed her to Melissa's tangled body, arm bent backward and behind her. Karina pointed to her arm. "It had to be bad to come true."

"What the fuck are you talking about?" Jay sobbed over Melissa's body.

"She's alive, isn't she?" Karina chewed a dirty thumbnail, hoping she was right.

Melissa twitched and groaned.

She looked to Jay, who held Melissa in a loving embrace. "You should go down the mountain. There's a ranger at the campground who can help."

"I'm not leaving her. Can you go?"

"I can't do that."

"Why not?" Jay wiped snot away from her nose.

"Because I have to finish the story."

"What the hell are you talking about?" Jay seethed.

To the unseen shadow she shouted, "You wanna know what happens next?"

She turned to Jay and Melissa and felt the truth of what she wanted to do at her lips. It pressed against her, wanting out. She needed to expel her secret darkness.

"I'm going to the summit, where I'll take in the view like I used to do with my father, like I meant to do with my family. And then I am going to throw myself from the boulder at the tippy top and rid the world of the evil that has attached itself to me."

Jay remained silent. Her eyes were wide and worried like she was speaking with a psychopath. But that didn't matter. Karina needed to end this by making one final bad thing happen.

"It's not a far drop, but the rocks are jagged. They'll crack open my skull, and then break some ribs and fracture the rest of my bones to match my busted arm." Her nerves sparked at the thought of the same pain extending across her entire body. "I'll lie there in the rising sun, spine snapped, paralyzed, eyes bulging just like my son's were when he died. Exposed brain matter growing cold as vultures and crows circle above, waiting to feast on my flesh. All while I'm still alive and warm inside. That's I'm going to do."

A draining sensation flushed through Karina. A feeling of relief, like the darkness within sank to her toes and seeped into the diorite rock below. Karina didn't turn back to see Jay's expression. She grabbed a sapling and used it for support to climb the hill back up to the trail.

When she reached it, she let out a long, nervous breath, and set her sights on the summit and the end to her story.

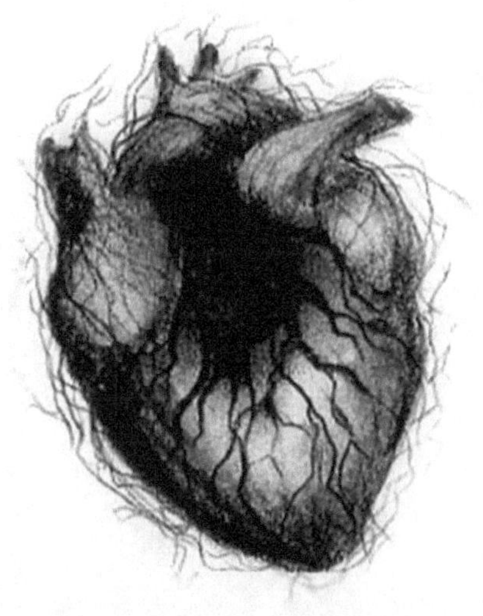

# CHAPTER 10

A calm settled over Karina. A sense of finality and acceptance that her pain and suffering would come to an end. Hellbent on free-falling from the top of the boulder and becoming sustenance for the vultures. It would hurt, and she feared that part of it, but the reward of stopping the shadow thing was worth it. She could finally silence her corrupt mind, denying her ragged heart one more beat, and once and for all allow the rotting corpses within her to bleed out.

She made it to the summit in an hour and a half. Her calves screamed. Thighs burned. Her broken arm burned like fire beneath the cast. Karina climbed the chiseled stone steps to a short path that wrapped around a huge outcrop of rock, and the shelter came into view.

The mountains in the distance were obscured by thick low clouds. More chiseled rock steps wrapped around boulders. No early morning hikers had made it to the top yet. She was alone and ready to realize the final scene.

She scrambled onto a boulder, shuffling closer to the far edge overlooking the valley. The foggy clouds below began to part. She should just fall into the mist and hope to plummet directly to her death, but the fog obscured the distance. She hesitated.

*Just get it over with.*

But something inside stopped her.

She didn't want to die. Not that it mattered. She'd already imagined it, so it was carved in stone as permanent as the diorite on which she stood.

She shuffled half a foot closer to the edge, the fog welcoming her.

Karina faced the valley, toes overhanging the edge of the rock. She closed her eyes and imagined what she'd pictured earlier.

"It's set in stone," Karina said.

Three specks at least a mile away soared in circles near the treetops below and she wondered if they were the birds that would feed on her ruined body. Fear replaced her confidence. The darkness was no longer calling. Below was a void and an uncertain end.

She took a few steps back, then blew all the air from her lungs. She pushed off her toes and ran toward the edge, but at the last moment, she skidded, pebbles sending an avalanche over the ledge. Karina dropped to the rock before her momentum carried her over. She collapsed, flattening her quaking body.

Why wasn't it happening? Why couldn't she just throw herself from the ledge? Karina lingered at the summit unable to finish what she came to do. Hours passed, and hikers came and went, while she waited for her courage to return, but it was lost. No matter how badly she wanted to put an end to it all, ultimately, the shadow would decide which of her stories it wanted.

Today wasn't her day to die, and no matter how badly she wanted it, ultimately the shadow would decide which of her stories it desired to manifest. Karina climbed back onto the boulder and looked out. She could breathe. For the first time since she'd lost them, the pressure of the darkness had eased. There was room for light.

Karina drove through Windsor on the last leg of her journey home. It was late, but she stopped to see her mother and the journal her father kept.

As her mom opened the front door, Karina spilled inside into an unplanned embrace.

Mom's arms were weak and reluctant to hug her back. "What? Are you okay?" She retreated for a better look. "You're a mess."

"Where is it?" Karina asked.

"The journal?"

Karina nodded.

"It's on the kitchen table."

Karina sat beside the spiral notebook with its bloody hockey mask cover. "You didn't know about this?"

She shook her head. "I found it in his studio. I hadn't been in there since..."

"It's been a year and you haven't been in his studio until now?"

Tears welled in Mom's eyes. "I couldn't." She brushed a stray hair from her brow. "Anyway, I was in there because I'm clearing it out."

"What are you doing with it?"

"Do you want any of it?"

"Yes!"

"Well, there's some of it that I'm going to sell, but the rest—"

"You can't sell them!"

"I need to. This may surprise you, but your father's obsession with horror art wasn't exactly paying all the bills. But he had fans. I can sell what's left and make enough to hold me over for a few months, along with my retirement checks."

Karina didn't know what to say, so she switched her attention from her mother to the notebook. She ran her fingers along the surface, trying to remember him.

"It was tucked in one of his desk drawers under some invoices. And when I read it..."

"That's an invasion of his privacy, Mom."

"Don't wax superior with me, young lady! You've got a lot of nerve coming in here and judging me, when *you*..."

"When I what? When I imagined my husband and my kid die a horrible death and it came true? When a man with an axe tried to kill me after I thought about it for only a second? When my neighbor down the street hung himself because I was annoyed with him and wished he would?" She trembled, spewing it all onto the floor at her mother's feet to be judged. To be chastised.

Mom tugged her collar. "I told you that kind of darkness shouldn't be inside anyone. It festers. It spreads. It's evil. I'm getting all of your father's hateful art out of my house. There's no place for it here."

Karina opened the journal and skimmed the pages. Blue pen scratching out his thoughts.

"March 31. That's where he talks about how he's afraid of having a stroke."

Karina skimmed through the pages. She needed to take it home and read it thoroughly. As she continued to flip, the handwriting changed. It suddenly became messy and child-like.

Mom sat beside her, twisting her necklace between pinched fingers. "That was after his stroke. If you keep reading. If you can read it. It's very messy. He was seeing things that weren't there. I didn't know he was suffering like that..." Mom's chin trembled as she fought the building tears. "I didn't know." Mom pushed away from the table. "Look at his last entry..."

Karina turned the page to shaky crude lines made into nearly illegible words:

*I have not drawn in weeks and I must. Sometimes I wish my heart would just stop so I could finally be free of this prison of a body.*

Mom wiped her nose with a tissue and sighed. "Hallucinations of a dark figure, too. It's all in there."

Karina closed the book, as if she could trap the darkness inside. "A dark figure?"

"I don't know. Whatever it was must've been evil, and it's inside you as well."

"What do I do?"

"I suggest you find a way to control this before. I can't lose you, too."

"I've been trying! I was so close to having it do whatever I wanted."

Mom's shoulders fell and she backed away. "What are you saying?"

"My imagination. The things that happen. When I was in the mountains, I made something happen. Something amazing. Something *impossible.*"

"Karina, no. This is dark magic. It's the devil or something very, very evil. You have to purge this from—"

"No!" Karina clutched the notebook to her chest. "This is it! This is what I need. Don't you see?"

"If you continue down this path, I can't...I can't allow this evil in my house."

"Mom, it's not evil! It's just me!"

She gestured for Karina to leave. "But you are immersed in a darkness that I can't be around."

Karina stepped onto her mother's front porch.

Mom's eyes were glassy, reflecting the pitch black of the world outside. Her lips trembled. "I let your dad's darkness take over my life for too long. And I won't have it any longer. My pastor agrees. We are here for you when you're willing to receive help. Until then, I won't speak with you anymore."

"Mom..." Her mother closed the door, leaving Karina shattered and alone in her world of darkness. She wished her mom would choke on her words. Let the words hang in the back of her throat and swell so she couldn't breathe. The imagined vision of her mother's death played in her head, but as she listened by the door for the sound of her mother dropping dead, the porch lights flicked off and all she could hear was the shuffling of Mom's feet moving out of earshot.

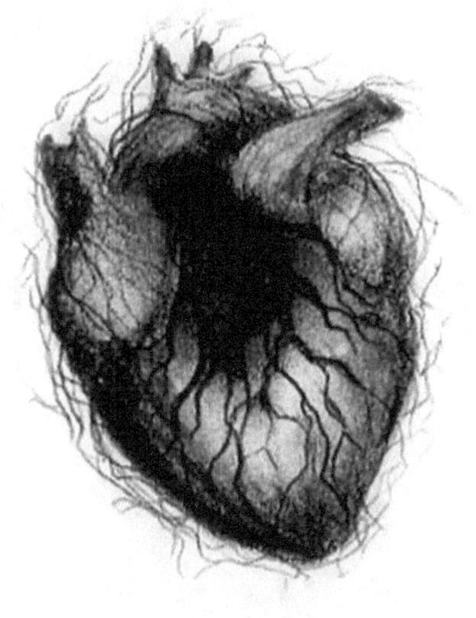

# CHAPTER 11

At home, she lay in Xander's bed, still dirty from her trip to the mountains, but too weak to shower. Xander's sketchbook and her father's journal weighed upon her chest. No matter how hard she pushed, they couldn't ease the aching and malignant pain beneath her flesh. She closed her eyes and pictured Xander lying beside her. She pet his mousey curls, calming his nerves. She coddled him the way she should have when he was a baby. She nursed his woeful cries with love instead of cautious distance. But it was too late for that. She'd failed at motherhood, and she'd never get a chance to right those mistakes.

Out of the corner of her eye, she expected to see the shadow looming, but it wasn't there. The air was metallic like a storm, like blood, like her tongue on a 9-volt battery. It was the darkness within her spilling out. It was her shadow self-materializing from grief, from despair, from the horrors trapped inside her. And it was time to face them.

Karina left Xander's sketchbook on his bed and carried her dad's journal to the kitchen island, claiming a stool. She opened it and plunged into the darkest places of his mind.

She stayed up all night reading it, deciphering what he'd written and matching it to the calendar with the dates of his stroke and heart attack. He only wrote in his journal about once a week, and every other entry he mentioned a fear of dying too young. He spilled his heart onto the page in ink and worried, even though healthy, that he'd have a stroke like his father had and leave his family without making things right. His words were dark and sad. Every few pages, Karina stepped away to compose herself.

Mom had known he was depressed. She didn't understand the extent of his suffering. He kept it bottled up inside so it wouldn't leak and spill into his marriage.

The next day, Karina returned to Onyx Oracle & Oddities in Norfolk to speak with Van.

"Karina," Clara said, coming around the counter. Her face was bright and fresh, a stark contrast to the dull, dirty exterior Karina knew she possessed. "You're back."

She cradled her father's journal against her chest. As the store's calming notes of lavender hit her senses, exhaustion finally struck.

Van entered from the back storage room. They locked eyes with Karina and drifted closer. "Did you look into shadow work?"

"A little. Did Clara tell you about what I made happen?"

Van crossed their arms. "It was intriguing, but I'm not one to believe just anything."

"I can make things happen. I've done it. It's not consistent though. It's not everything. But my dad could do it too. It's all in here. He imagined the first stroke."

Clara threw her head back with a loud, groaning sigh.

Karina continued. "He wrote about having a stroke, and then it happened. Then there were no journal entries for a while because he was recovering. But then another entry months later. His handwriting was chaotic because he hadn't regained full function. But he wrote that he missed painting..." She flipped open the book toward the middle, close to his last entry, where the handwriting changed. "Here...he kept seeing a, I think it says *dark figure*. It's all in here! How he used to make things happen when he was younger. But then found an outlet for his darkness."

Clara smiled at a customer who entered and then lowered her voice. "This doesn't make sense, Karina." She leaned closer. "Seriously, when have you showered or changed your clothes last?"

Van extended their hands to request permission to hold the book.

Karina relinquished control.

Van flipped pages, chewing their lip, brow furrowed. "The thought form of your inner darkness..."

"No," Clara held out a hand. "Don't encourage this fantasy anymore. Look at her. She's unraveling." She faced Karina. "*You're unraveling*. Listen to yourself. *Look* at yourself."

"I know." Karina felt her crazed eyes, tired and piercing. She knew she was still dirty from the mountains and appeared frazzled. Her lips were scabbed over where they'd chapped and bled. But it all was starting to make sense.

Van nodded, leaning in and talking though their teeth. "Clara, this is stuff I didn't even know could happen."

"Because it *can't* happen." She picked up her phone. "I know you're a grown woman, Karina, but I really think I should call your mother."

The absurdity made Karina burst into laughter. Her smile stretched her dry lips, breaking the scabs and drawing new blood. "Mom thinks I'm evil and doesn't want anything to do with me."

"For Christ's sake, she's a big part of this problem. If she were supportive when you needed—"

"No, hear me out. What Van said about the manifestation of your inner darkness. Think about it. Dad suffered depression, just like me. We were both very private with our feelings."

"You both bottled your feelings," Clara said.

Van's eyes widened. "And the shadow self doesn't like being bottled. It needs to be dealt with."

Clara tilted her head, exasperated. "But you said yourself, Van, the shadow self is a philosophical thing. It's not a real life entity."

"Maybe it can be. And if so, what would it do if it's caged for too long, pressure building with each trauma, each heartbreak, each bottled emotion?"

Van leaned in. "Your dad expelled his demons, metaphorical demons, onto the canvas. That was his outlet. That's why his shadow self didn't manifest."

"Until he had a stroke." Karina whispered.

"And he couldn't release those feelings anymore. He couldn't let those dark images free."

Clara shook her head. "No. Your dad had this journal as an outlet and, it didn't work. These theories aren't holding up."

Van and Karina stood over the open journal.

Clara leaned on her elbows from the opposite side. "I can't condone you looking into this any longer. I can't watch you destroy what's left of your life."

"There is nothing left!" Karina snapped, relieving pressure. The draining sensation tingled in her toes. The feeling she had when she'd stood by Jay and Melissa and told them precisely how she'd kill herself. "I have to go." Karina scooped up her father's journal and hurried away.

"Karina!" Clara called after her but stayed behind the counter.

The door jingled as she swung it open and left behind her only friend.

The emptiness of home ate her alive. The shadow thing hadn't appeared in days, and she began to wonder if she'd left it in the mountains. She finally made an appearance at work without bothering to alert anyone. Surprised faces greeted her. Tilted heads, pinched eyebrows, and tight lips expressed confusion masked as concern. They were smart enough to leave her be. Brenda, the reliable temp being considered as a permanent replacement, seemed disappointed that she was back.

The clackity clack and hissing of the production floor quieted Karina's mind. The hot stench of melting plastic overpowered the metallic tang of the shadow figure who seemed to be gone for good. A new machine operator stood at the conveyor of the stapler case line, pulling parts from the belt and boxing them. Karina, upon doing her inspection rounds, pulled a set from the belt and noted a thin line of flash along the edge.

The molten plastic material had done what it was supposed to do. It filled two halves of a mold which were pressed tightly together. When the plastic is too hot, or if there's too much pressure, it will seep out the seams between the mold halves, creating a thin line of plastic excess.

Razor sharp, and far too much to pass inspection, this flaw in production was bad enough that the entire box of stapler casings would have to be sorted through for flaws. Arguing with the foreman wasn't something she felt like doing, but the job is the job, and the parts couldn't be shipped.

"They're out of specification."

"I can't run them any cooler or the mold won't fill out." He removed a trucker hat, slicked back his receding hairline and returned it to his sweaty head.

"Maybe it's the pressure."

He looked at her through pinched eyebrows. "I checked the pressure."

Karina sighed, "All I know is they won't pass inspection like this. Someone will cut themselves on that."

She nearly choked on her words, drowning the memory of her son's lacerated tongue, of blood pouring from his mouth. She stepped to the next machine to gather another set of parts for inspection.

Karina wasn't sure if she was measuring the parts and recording correctly, but she pushed through the hours anyway. It was as if her mind had left her body to handle the mundane task.

"Check out this beauty." The foreman hung inside the quality control room with new stapler case in his hand.

The flash had been resolved.

"Pressure?" she asked.

"Timing. The mold was closed for a split second too long. Too much material being pumped in and nowhere for it to go but out the seams."

The mold could only take so much material before the hot molten excess squeezed out and caused problems.

When her father poured his imagination onto the page and sent it for others to share, he could fill back up with more darkness. But when he stopped purging the material, the mold stopped opening and the darkness squeezed out the edges into reality.

It'd been a few days since she'd seen the shadow thing, and none of her accidentally imagined scenes had come true. Not when she pictured her mother choking to death, or when she envisioned Clara's store burning down. Not since she stood on the mountain and released some of her rage, her feelings, her darkness into words which were absorbed by the hiking women. Her mold opened that day and finally released the material the way it was supposed to. And now she needed to wait until it filled up again. The timing wasn't right yet.

Karina quit without notice and went home to sit on her couch and wait for the darkness to return. With her curtains drawn tight, she locked her doors and conjured the most negative thoughts she could imagine. Dad's journal and Xander's sketchbook sat on the coffee table in front of her. The injustice of their deaths over something as innocuous as bottling feelings only stoked the flames of fury within her. Dad died because Mom wouldn't let him draw. And Xander died because of Karina's lifelong need to keep her feelings to herself, a result of her mother's upbringing. Helen never allowed her family to share their darkness, and so it seeped out as flash, slicing their lives apart.

The anger began to swell, but Karina wasn't ready to release her fury. She didn't want to open her mold and avoid the manifestation of what lurked within. Karina sat in her dark and empty home, hungry, lonely, infuriated, and she bottled it as tight as she could, awaiting the shadow to squeeze out of her once again.

# CHAPTER 12

Several weeks passed, and Karina refused to speak with anyone. She forced down enough food and water to keep from passing out and waited. The vile sludge of her guilt and anger and regret filled her soul until the pressure was so high it had to escape. She allowed every negative thought, every dark imagined thing to run through her brain.

She pictured accidents at work, explosions and molten plastic leaks. Terrible tragedies she tried not to dwell on for too long. She ran through scenarios of vehicles flipping over on the highway. A minivan careening off the bridge and into the Elizabeth River. She wondered if another mother could handle the trauma of losing everyone she loved in a single moment. Neighbors walked by as she lurked hidden in shadow, watching from a narrow opening in the curtain. She pictured dogs turning on their owners, gnawing into legs, and she imagined the ache in her broken arm becoming so damned unbearable that she'd have to saw the damn thing off because of a gangrenous spread. But none of it came true. She jammed a ruler inside her cast to help scratch the incessant itchiness within. She'd missed her follow-up appointment weeks ago but couldn't live with herself if she left her house and missed the opportunity to release the shadow again.

At night, she sat with Xander's sketchbook, focusing on his hate—FUCK YOU MOM FUCK YOU MOM FUCK YOU MOM FUCK YOU MOM. Finally, while lying in his bed and staring at his ceiling, long-reaching shadows shifted and moved. No movement outside, no curtain blowing in a breeze. A source-less shadow came alive as massive ink legs clawed the ceiling. Tears welled in her eyes, but she widened them, fought the burn and refused to let them escape. Nothing. Not a single emotion was allowed to leave her body.

The days went on and an ache pressed at her ribcage. Shadowed hands squeezed between ribs, desperate to abandon her prison of pain. What if she were to cut open her throat, let scarlet horrors spill from the confines of her flesh? An exodus of darkness and demise. A release, but then she'd be dead, lying in a crimson puddle of potential, rather than making something of it all.

More days passed and she wondered if she should give up on her attempt to bring back the shadow figure at all. She seemed so close, catching glimpses of dark splotches in the corners that vanished when viewed head-on. Perhaps she was too broken, mind lost in an abyss of grief from which there'd never be an escape.

Finally, one night, while she lay in her own bed staring at the ceiling, she noticed movement in the corner of her eye. A black void, darker than the deepest recess of outer space. It swelled in the corner. She didn't look at it directly, but it stood watching her. Tiny static sparks of lightning burst in its black, cloudy presence.

The taste of iron filled the room. It kissed her lips as if her husband were with her, reaching from beyond the grave, beyond the velvet-lined casket, through the fresh soil. He came back to her, metallic elements of the dirt entwined with his decomposing flesh. And he kissed her. She closed her eyes and welcomed him home like he'd been on another deployment and finally pulled into port. The good times, the laughter, the late-night talks, morning breath smiles, the *light,* tried to enter, but she snuffed it out. Cut the power at its source so he'd linger a little longer with her in the darkness. The shadow feared the light.

The inky splotch in the corner swelled up the walls of her room, reaching to the ceiling, then stretched outward. A black mass birthed from the touch of Gavin's lips. Twig-like shadows scribbled overhead, mimicking Xander's art. Massive, insect-like legs skittered and scuttled. Its two-dimensional shape lowered from the ceiling, creating a shadow of its own. Lines scratched in and out of existence, jerking across the ceiling until it was directly above her. A sharpening point on one of its appendages descended. Karina's fear petrified her in place, but when the pointed tip of the appendage was so close she could smell the ink, she flipped herself out of bed and crashed to the floor on her hands and knees. Karina scrambled out of her son's room, slamming the door shut behind.

As she pressed her back against the door, imagining the thing trapped inside, too large to squeeze beneath the crack, a smile threatened for a fraction of a second and then was swallowed by the gravity of the moment.

For the next few days, Karina focused on writing. It was clunky and awkward when she sat at the keyboard, unsure how to start, how to tell a tale worth reading. She hadn't written a story in years, but it didn't matter. She was writing for herself.

She pictured them. Her dad, her husband, her son. The three most important people in her life. She used to imagine their corpses rotting away inside of her. Carrying their ghosts around like a cement block tied to her ankle while she fought to stay afloat. But now, she released them onto the page. They were no longer her burden to carry. No longer her regret, her guilt, her anguish. They would be here with her, but as separate entities. Alive and haunting her from the outside, rather from within.

She wrote about Gavin first. The man who, when her father abandoned her for the darkness, was there with a torch to keep her from falling into the abyss at her feet. She scratched out words to mark her anguish, her loss, and her utter terror as her husband clawed his way out of the grave, because he wasn't really dead. Dripping with embalming fluid, stench of rot and petrichor clinging to crumbling bits of earth and flesh as they fell from his body. Karina imagined herself in the shower when he would arrive. The cold, sterile, white tile a backdrop to her loneliness. A shadow would loom behind the curtain, but this time when she opened it, there'd be no inky black nebula. No ghost or metallic presence. It would be Gavin, exhumed and half-alive. Her heart raced imagining his deceased body stumbling across the bathroom floor, leaving a trail of dirt and decay. She'd step aside and let him join her, while the aroma of petrichor and a hint formaldehyde would plume from his body. Laced among the scents would be his aftershave. The memory of his old self would excite her flesh into goosebumps despite the scouring heat of the water pounding against her back and splattering onto his face. Karina slid his black jacket from his shoulders, loosened the tie from his neck; but before she could remove his shirt, Gavin placed his hands on her waist and lowered himself to his knees. His hands squeezed her back in a loving and desperate embrace, and she knew that he appreciated her for bringing him back to her. His lips dragged across her wet belly, and he grabbed her ass, backing her against the wall. He plunged lower, kissing along her bikini line until he lifted her leg and she placed it on the ledge of the tub. Vomit boiled in her stomach, but she trapped it in the back of her throat and swallowed. She couldn't bear to look at his decrepit skull and gray decaying brain matter. Gavin dove his face into her, and she sparked alive with ecstasy and disgust. Her fingers clenched handfuls of hair that tore from his loosely stitched skull. His tongue plunged into her labial folds, and she threw her head back, toes curling. One arm braced itself on a ledge, knocking the shampoo into the tub. From her angle, looking down, it was her Gavin, but his skull had spilled open, brain matter bubbled to the surface and dribbled into the shower basin.

The throbbing ache between her legs longed for him and each day she wrote herself to orgasm. Karina typed furiously for hours every day, page after page, imagining a life where she could have her family back. Her keystrokes were clumsy with the weight of her cast restricting her movements. She couldn't risk leaving the house and bringing her darkness out in the world, but enough time had passed she needed to consider removing it on her own. Gavin had plenty of small saws out in the garage.

She opened the door from the kitchen to the garage and flipped the light switch. Gavin's wood-shop was pristine. The hand saws hung in order of size and type on a pegboard behind his bench. Hanging on the last hook was the chainsaw he'd used for the bear carving. A story idea struck her, and she ran to grab her laptop so she could work on it where inspiration had struck.

Sickening anticipation pulled at her insides as she finished the story that had to have been dark enough to bring Gavin back. Karina slept at her keyboard. When she woke, she drank bitter, cold black coffee, then she typed some more. She'd see her loves for moments; Dad would paint beside her while she typed, and Gavin would work on the bear carving he never finished. Xander would sit in the corner, sketching. Were they mere apparitions of her imagination or did she conjure them back into reality? Afraid they'd disappear if she looked, Karina kept typing.

Until a knock at the door broke her from her creative spell.

She was alone in her bedroom. The curtains were drawn, but daylight shone through the opening. The screen's rectangle burned into her retinae as she broke away and staggered down the hall toward the front door. Her hair was a tangled nest of greasy curls. The mirror she passed reflected sunken eyes and dull skin in need of hydration. Several cracks in her lips had scabbed over. Karina couldn't remember if she drank anything other than coffee, or when she'd eaten last.

A second knock at the door sounded like a gunshot through her dead home. Her head throbbed as she peeked into the glaring world to see her mother and Clara standing together.

Karina tried to feign some appearance of normalcy. She ran her fingers through her hair, residue clogging her nails. She adjusted her low ponytail and patted the skin under her eyes, then opened the door.

The rising sun assaulted her. The aroma of fresh spring rain carried into the house, reminiscent of mountain fog.

Clara didn't say a word, but the expression she couldn't hide announced her concern. Her nose twitched.

Mom's face soured. She pushed by Karina and charged into the house. "It's foul in here."

Karina did not respond. Getting her mother in the house had been part of her story. It was finally happening, but she didn't anticipate Clara coming along.

# Chapter 13

Using her eyes Karina tried to signal Clara to leave. She shouldn't have come, but Clara entered and closed the door behind.

Mom raided the refrigerator, sniffing for the source of the smell that Karina no longer noticed.

"What is that smell?"

Clara's lips pursed. "This is kind of an intervention, Karina."

"I'm fine." Her voice was weak, having not been used in days, or had it been weeks?

Clara's eyes traveled up and down Karina's physique. "You're not taking care of yourself, so you're not fine."

"Is it the trash?" Mom lifted the lid to the can drawing in a whiff.

Clara threw her head back. "Some rotten food in the fridge is hardly a pressing issue, Helen!"

Karina's mom lowered the lid and crossed her arms. Her chin lifted and her judgmental eyes traveled down her nose at Karina. "We're worried about you."

"Do you want some coffee?" Karina moved into the kitchen, bare feet cold on the hard floor. Sweatpants sagging from at least a week's worth of wear. How long had it been?

"I'll get it," Helen said and put a hand on Karina's back. "Go sit down, dear."

Karina let her mother's hand linger on her shoulder blade for a moment, then she jerked herself away. "Careful Mom. Wouldn't want anything bad to happen, you know?"

Helen's hand cautiously lifted, and she backed away as if Karina was a ticking bomb. She fumbled for the cross around her neck.

Clara put herself between Karina and her mother. "I'll get the coffee. Helen, have a seat. Van will be here soon."

"Van?"

"Shall we sit out on the back porch? Get some fresh air? Talk this out?" Helen asked.

"There's nothing to talk about," Karina said, taking a seat at the counter.

"How've you been doing?" Clara asked, emptying the sludge from the coffee pot.

"I've been writing."

Helen stiffened in her seat.

Clara rinsed the pot. "Journaling can be very therapeutic. Is it helping?"

"It's more like fiction." Karina let out a huff with a chuckle. "Horror fantasy, I guess." She glared at her mother.

Helen's back straightened like a board. "Why on earth would you start—"

"Because I have to!" Karina charged.

Helen held her ground by the door. "Your demented imagination is what got you into this mess."

"*You* got us into this mess. *You* made all this happen. Don't you see your influence?"

"On whom?" Helen asked.

"On me and Dad! You killed Dad the moment you took his paintbrushes away."

"Don't you talk to me that way."

A thump from the garage silenced the house.

Clara and Mom's attention turned to the adjoining door.

"What was that?" Clara asked.

As Clara moved toward the door, Karina grabbed her wrist and shook her head. "You should leave."

"I'm not going anywhere."

"It was just supposed to be her."

Clara eyed the door as Helen approached.

Mom reached a hand for the doorknob. "Hello?" She turned to Karina. "It smells like a dead animal in there." She covered her mouth and nose with a cupped hand.

Mom turned the knob and poked her head into the garage.

Panic set in and Karina didn't know what else to do other than tell Clara the horrors that could unfold if she stayed. Telling her would save Clara, but it would also save her mother.

Karina whispered out of earshot of Helen. "Clara, you need to go before the corpses of everyone I love grab you by the throat and choke you to death. You need to leave before their dead eyes set their gaze upon you and drag you six feet into the soil. Or before they light your body ablaze with gasoline and a match. There are so many ways to die, and I don't know how it'll happen until I think of it."

"What the fuck is wrong with you?" Clara's eyes went back to the garage as Helen released the door and backed away from the darkness.

"If I tell you, it can't happen." She grabbed Clara's shoulders, but her friend yanked away.

A knock at the front door came the moment Mom released a guttural screech. She bent in half, retreating from the garage as a figure staggered into the light.

Dad stood framed in the doorway. Half of his was face numb and lifeless. Drool dribbled from his lips. Pale gray, mummified skin stretched across his bony features.

A paintbrush was clutched in one hand and splotches of black and red dappled his blue and orange tracksuit. It was the only way she could bring him back, partially paralyzed from stroke, unable to speak. She needed to envision him exactly the way she never wanted to see him. The most horrifying image of her father was when he lost all control of himself. She'd imagined him standing beside her, paintbrush in hand, crude strokes assaulting the canvas as she typed the story of his revenge. He'd never died at all, but instead had stowed away in her garage, creating, raging and scheming. He'd painted how he'd take a tube of cadmium red and squeeze it down his wife's throat until she filled with it. Her insides would bulge with paint, body convulsing from the toxicity.

But mom was feisty and wouldn't give up without a fight. She already had a knife in hand from the butcher block. "You're not my husband!"

"Mom," Karina said. "Put the knife down."

Clara's eyes filled with tears. "What did you do?"

"I saved them," Karina whispered.

Mom held the knife loosely, sobbing as her late husband approached, a large tube of cadmium red in his meaty fist.

Clara grabbed Karina's shirt collar and backed her against the wall. "What's he doing?"

"Karina!" Mom sputtered.

Clara shoved her, pressing her fist into her collarbone. "What the fuck, Karina?!"

Karina's shoulders dropped, knowing she'd lose even more people if she let her dad continue. She didn't really want her mother to die. She simply wanted to teach her a lesson. "He's going to take that tube of paint and shove it down her throat until she chokes to death."

Mom's sobs intensified and she dropped to her knees.

Clara let Karina go, eyes wild and lost. She rushed over to Helen who wobbled, staggering like she was about to faint. Clara caught her in time, grabbed the knife from Helen's hand, and lowered her safely to the ground.

"Get the fuck back, dude," Clara swung at the air between her and Karina's father.

Karina sighed. "Well, he's not going to do it now, because I told you the story."

"Tell him to back off!"

But this dad wasn't Karina's quiet-minded father who did whatever he was told. He was a new creation, a violent and vengeful force that was not to be fucked with. He jolted forward, fist raised, but Clara was too quick for Dale. Karina had no time to imagine the next scenario.

"Van! Get help!"

Karina turned to see Van standing by the front door, pinned by fear.

Clara swiped the knife at Dale, blade slashing through his tracksuit with ease, parting the flesh beneath. His skin opened, spilling not blood, but a thick black sludge. It poured out of him like a waterfall, and misted into a black nebula sparking with electrical life. The cloud rolled over the body of Karina's unconscious mother. It dusted past Clara who seemed frozen in shock or fear or some emotion Karina didn't care to empathize with at the moment. All that mattered was the darkness that was her father came back to her. It coated her toes and climbed her legs, seeping into pores until it filled her up with the sludge of what was once his rotting corpse.

Clara dropped the knife and shook Helen until she woke. By the front door, Van stood with their mouth agape. Eyes wide as two full moons.

"Helen," Clara said. "We have to go."

She helped Helen to her feet and kept a watchful eye on Karina as she neared the front door.

Clara looked back to Karina and shook her head. "Stay the fuck away from us all."

Karina's body ached with the loss of her father, but filled with a darkness most welcome.

"You do the same!"

Van's curiosity kept them in the house after Clara and Helen escaped. They didn't say anything at first, but Karina understood they were there for knowledge, not to help her.

"Did you see him?" Karina asked.

Van nodded.

"I made it happen. I brought him back."

Van's voice tremored. "You manifested something, but I don't think it was really *him*."

"I don't care what you think." Spite and fury rose in her gut, climbing up her throat like a beast wanting to slaughter anyone who tried to take away her family again. "Get out before it comes for you, too."

"I'm just trying to help."

Karina let out a sigh, afraid to release the thing within. She growled. "Get out!"

Like a wild animal, Karina lay panting, curled on the kitchen floor, mourning her father's death once again. Her broken arm lay crushed beneath her weight. As she lay snarling and crying, another sound roared to life in the garage. She jumped to her feet. A motor ran inside the garage, the small engine sound of Gavin's chainsaw. Karina eased toward the doorway and snuck a peek inside. He wore red flannel and jeans. The fourteen-inch chainsaw carved strategic pieces away from the unfinished bear. Sawdust spewed tiny motes into the air, landing in the exposed brain that oozed out of his broken skull.

He looked exactly as she'd written him. Karina softly approached from the side, terrified of what was about to happen, but it was the only way to keep him here.

"Hi, stranger," she said.

"How's my salty sailor?" Gavin smiled; morning breath replaced by decay. He raised his chainsaw and asked. "Need help cutting that thing off?"

She lay her casted forearm flat on the bench and turned her head away.

The motor roared. The vibrations of teeth cutting through plaster rattled her bones for only a second before giving way to the searing pain of metal tearing through flesh and bone.

Karina collapsed, shrieking in blinding pain, but Gavin pinned her arm in place. The last tendon snapped and she fell to the cement floor, leaving her severed arm in the bulk of the cast up on the bench. Blood splattered onto the floor, Gavin's pant legs, and across Karina's face. It reminded her of her last moments with Xander when he spat blood, laughing in the back seat. Gavin hit the switch on the chainsaw and set it safely beside her dismembered forearm. He pulled his belt from his pants and tied a tourniquet at her elbow.

Karina bit a hole through her fragile lips, fighting the intensifying agony. Vision tunneled so narrow she wished she could pass out, but she wasn't allowed the pleasure of sleep in this reality. Gavin pulled the branding iron from coals, which she didn't realize he'd already heated. The red, glowing anchor came toward her, and Gavin pressed it into her bleeding stub. The stench of burning flesh hit her nose, and just before passing out, she heard her mother's voice ask:

*What are you going to do now?*

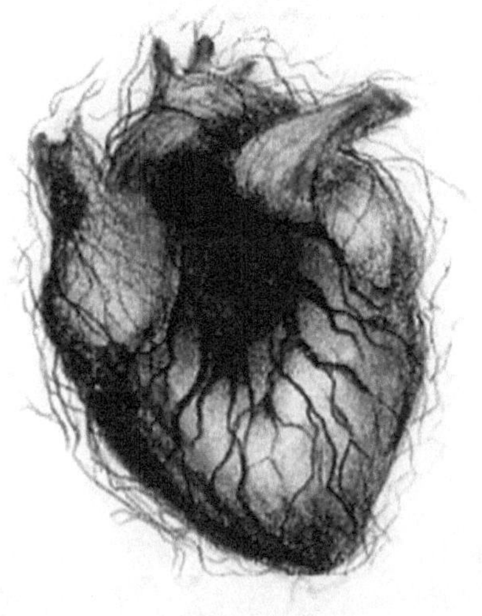

# CHAPTER 14

A small log house in the mountains became the place Karina called home. She'd sought out the most secluded place she could afford after the sale of her home. It was cut off from people and the expectations they had of her.

Adjusting to life with a single arm became easier after the cauterized wound healed. Weeks of bandages and ointments and more over the counter pain medicine than her liver should've been able to handle. But she couldn't go to the hospital. What would she tell them? It'd be a one-way ticket to the psych ward.

She lit a fire and sat at her computer to write the stories she'd always wanted to tell. Her father's art, which she bought anonymously from her mother, adorned the walls of her writing room. Maybe someday she'd submit stories to the same horror magazines her father's art used to grace. It'd be a good way to keep her darkness from squeezing out, becoming a sharp jagged ridge of flash which could lacerate the world. If she'd learned anything from all this, it was that sometimes she needed to share the burden of her darkness with others. It eased the pressure and the load she carried.

But first, before sharing, she'd be happy to hone her skills. And here in the middle of the woods, alone, she didn't have to worry about hurting anyone but herself.

Karina finished a short story and switched off her computer. Across the narrow hallway, she opened the door to Xander's bedroom. She'd decorated it with his things and the artwork from their old home. He sat on his bed, almost fully formed. The day before, he'd been a scribble of lines, black and red. A shadowy thing in human form. But today, after a full day of writing, Xander was taking shape. His face was crimson and wet with the blood from his injuries. It poured from an unknown source. His eyes refused to meet with hers as she beside him. She placed a hand on his back and leaned her head on her son's shoulder. Since they'd moved to the house, Xander had done some decorating of his own. FUCK YOU MOM FUCK YOU MOM FUCK YOU MOM was scrawled across his walls in defiance of her love. But she was okay with him hating her. She was okay with him being whoever he wanted to be. She kissed his blood-soaked cheek and tried to meet his lifeless eyes. Xander pulled away, shuffled toward the window, but the chain around his ankle was bolted to the floor. Karina's chin trembled and her teeth chattered, but she whispered, "I love you, baby boy. I always have. I just didn't know how to show you. I didn't know how to love you. But I'm learning. I promise I'll do better this time."

Xander picked up his black marker and continued where he'd left off, scratching letters on the drywall and across posters of his art... FUCK YOU MOM FUCK YOU MOM...

Karina's heart tremored, but she knew with time he'd come around. She had all the time in the world now. She backed out of his room and locked the door.

In her bedroom, she wiped her tears and found her strength. Karina undressed and wrapped a robe around her naked body before stepping into the bathroom where the shower had already started. Hot steam filled the tiny ensuite. Behind the curtain, Gavin awaited her. She let her robe slide from her shoulders and stepped toward the scent of petrichor and decay.

Here, she'd live in ecstasy and disgust. She'd fill herself with love and anguish, with fantasy and fear. For Karina, there would never be a void left behind by those she loved, because all she had to do was fill it up with whatever she wished. So long as those fantasies were born from the darkness within.

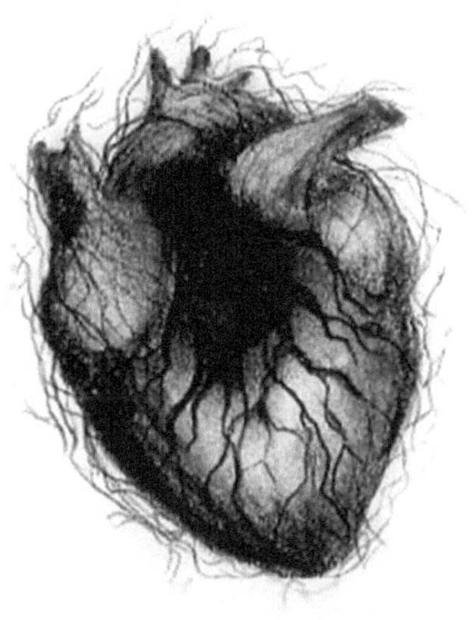

# Acknowledgements

*In Excess of Dark* originally released in March 2024 with a small press that has since shuttered its doors. I am incredibly thankful to L.C. Marino and L.P. Hernandez at Sobelo Books for believing in this bizarre story, for allowing space to include my illustrations, and for working around my insanely tight timeline for its re-release.

This book spawned from two different story ideas fusing together after a camping trip to the Blue Ridge Mountains. Thanks to the Peaks of Otter Campground and their primitive campsites, I had quiet solitude in the wilderness that conjured some of the imagery in this book. Particularly, the campground bathroom scene.

To my mom, Donna, who has been incredibly supportive since my first penned story on lined paper, thank you for reminding me often in my teen years that my dreams "had a way of coming true". Looking back, I recognize now that it was mostly incidents of déjà vu, but I remember vividly the look of worry in your eyes when I'd tell you about one of my weird dreams. You still look at me like I'm weird, but I think that may be for other reasons now.

Thank you to Laurel Hightower for your support and friendship. You made an excellent reading partner when I first shared a blip of this book with the world at Authorcon in 2023, and I'm so glad you were one of the first people to read it. It's been wonderful working with you on other projects over the past year, and I hope to work with you plenty more down the road.

To Ben Errington, for creating cover art for this book when I didn't even really know what I wanted. It is weird and colorful and absolutely perfect.

When the future of this book was unclear, I had some valuable conversations with many authors who helped me in making decisions about what would happen next. To name a few: Thank you, Gemma Amor, Brian Keene, Steve Stred, John Durgin, Yolanda Sfetsos, and Briana Morgan.

And to all the authors who offered blurbs and more, Todd Keisling, Kealan Patrick Burke, and Eric LaRocca: this writing community wouldn't be what it is without the kindness of authors offering to help others.

I hear it all the time, and experience it daily: *writing is a solitary business*. And while I may spend hours alone scheming, writing, and creating... with friends, family, and the horror community, I never really feel all that alone here in the suffocating darkness.

# Quick Favor

Thank you so much for dedicating your time to reading this book! May I ask a quick favor?

Please take a moment to leave a review on Amazon, Goodreads, or wherever you purchased the book. Your words have power. Your review can help this book haunt more people. We appreciate you!

# About the Author

Red Lagoe grew up on 80s horror and carried her paranoia of slashers and sewer creatures into adulthood. She is the author of the forthcoming novel, *Bloodstains by Gaslight* (Brigids Gate Press 2024). She has authored three horror collections including *Impulses of a Necrotic Heart*, *Lucid Screams*, and *Dismal Dreams*.

Red is the editor of the anthology *Nightmare Sky: Stories of Astronomical Horror*. As a staff writer for Crystal Lake Publishing's *Still Water Bay* series, she authored several contributing stories, and dozens of her other short stories have been published in various anthologies.

When Red is not creating, you may find her falling into a pit of despair, enveloped by an all-consuming darkness. Or she may be kayaking with her family, walking her dog, or lounging beneath a starry sky with a telescope.